JUSTICE FORGOTTEN

A Novel

Bill Jack

Chapbook Press

Schuler Books
2660 28th Street SE
Grand Rapids, MI 49512
(616) 942-7330
www.schulerbooks.com

Justice Forgotten

ISBN 13: 9781966196082

Library of Congress Control Number: 2024925699

Cover Art by Rebecca Sitterly

Printed in the United States.

DEDICATION

This novel is dedicated to the men and women of the Albuquerque Police Department Sex Crimes Unit who spend their careers risking their lives hunting down predators who sexually abuse men, women and children.

She never knew how he got into her apartment in Old Town and never would.

Her first memory out of a deep sleep was a cloth over her mouth and a knife at her throat. Her eyes focused on a ski mask and dark gloves holding the cloth and knife.

"Say one word or scream and you're dead." A Hispanic accent but nothing more.

Leslie slept naked and in seconds, he was on top of her and in her although she would later recall he was mostly flaccid. The act itself lasted only a short time and when he came, he let out a long breath of rancid decay and said,

"If you call the police – ever - you're a dead woman. I'll find you."

He got up from her bed and left as quietly as he had come in. She lay there for minutes with her mind trying to absorb what had just happened and grappling with the reality and the horror of it all. She thought of calling her boyfriend, but he was married and out of town with his family.

More minutes passed and she called her best friend, Jackie LaPointe, and told her what had happened.

"I'm right there, Leslie, I'm right there. Don't move."

And she was right there in minutes. Afraid to call the police in case her apartment was being watched by the rapist, Leslie and Jackie instead went to the University of New Mexico Emergency Room, got triaged and checked in, and taken by wheelchair into a bay. Jackie stayed with her. By now, she was nauseous, shaking and sobbing uncontrollably, and scared to death.

A nurse in UNM green scrubs came in, held Leslie's hand, and sat with her until she had settled down. Only a brief history because, after all, what was to be said other than she had been raped at knife point. The nurse gave her a pill to calm her nerves and left her alone with Jackie for a few minutes. They held hands and sat quietly listening to the sounds of the emergency room in the middle of the night.

The nurse came back in with a package that she described as a 'rape kit' designed to assess whether there was any physical damage and to take a vaginal swab to test for DNA. Once done, the nurse pulled the sheet up to Leslie's neck and left again.

Minutes passed and a uniformed policewoman came into the bay, introduced herself, took a history, made some notes, got the key to the apartment so officers could go through it and, on her way out, said,

"We'll be in touch."

That night, Leslie tried to sleep on Jackie's couch but not surprisingly there would be no sleep for either of them. The next morning, they went back to the apartment. The police had taken the bedding but, to

Leslie, the stench of the rapist's body and breath was still there. She went into the bathroom and vomited what little there was in her stomach. Leslie and Jackie went to the Manager's office, explained what happened, were met with sympathy by the woman manager who immediately found another apartment in one of the other complexes owned by the same company, and 48 hour later, Leslie Helm was in a new apartment. But it didn't matter.

She was never contacted by the Albuquerque Police Department.

Months went by and Leslie, despite the best efforts of her friends, slid into a life of despondency, despair and recurring nightmares about the attack. Her boyfriend who had promised he would leave his family and be with her, broke up with her because she was, as he put it, 'dirty.' He stayed with his wife and children.

Alcohol became her new best friend, clerical work at the University of New Mexico Law School Admissions office suffered, and life spiraled. Six months to the date of the rape, Leslie got into her bathtub, and slit her wrists.

Her landlord found her two days later when Leslie's boss called and said she hadn't been to work and wasn't returning phone calls or texts.

Before her body was transported back to her family in Nebraska where she was from, there was a small gathering of friends at a local bar. Jackie LaPointe, a recent graduate of the UNM Law School where she had met Leslie, gave as close to a eulogy as she could manage:

"Justice may have forgotten you, but we never will."

No arrest was ever made and, as far as Jackie and her friends knew, no investigation was ever even started.

Chapter One

The Past Uncovered

J.D. Rawlings, the brand-new District Attorney for the Second Judicial District, Bernalillo County, was in his new office at the Steven Schiff Office Building on his first day on the job and unpacking boxes of belongings that had come over from his office down the hall where he had been an Assistant District Attorney for several years.

He was trying to decide what pictures and plaques he should hang. Having served the people of the county for as long as he had, he had received any number of accolades in appreciation of the good work he had done, and they had hung proudly in his old office. Now, though, having been elected by 65% of the popular vote, he wondered if they really mattered. He pondered it for a moment and decided that if people didn't know who he was by now and if he didn't know who he was by now, all the plaques in the world weren't going to make a difference. He put them all back in the box and, in their place, he hung a couple of his favorite Southwestern art paintings from his old office and put a picture of his wife on his desk. He could fill more in later if the spirit moved him.

J.D. had been blessed with the looks of somebody who either should have been a Western movie star or a Texas Ranger in real life. Tall, rangy and thin as a rail, he had a face that, in the past, had attracted several women after his divorce but his heart had been captured once and for all by, of all things, a cop. Margaret Espinoza had risen through the ranks of the Albuquerque Police Department at a time when women were mostly objects of scorn, had endured years of sexism, and had proven time and again, she was every bit the cop her male colleagues were. And then some. She had survived the murder of her son and had finally been named Chief of the Homicide Division of the ABQ Police Department. She and J.D. had met working on a horrific murder case, had fallen in love, and had married. Each had never been happier.

J.D.'s picture hanging was interrupted by a knock on his door. His assistant, Julie Stahl, who had been with him for years and had followed him after the election, opened the door and announced that he had two calls waiting: The Mayor of Albuquerque and his wife.

"Not together, I hope."

"Nope. None of my business but I might start with the mayor. First day on the job after all. Line 2." She left and quietly closed the door behind her.

He nodded, put down the hammer and picture hangers, walked around his desk, picked up the phone and punched line two.

"Good morning, Your Honor."

"Have you seen the front page of the Albuquerque Journal this morning, J.D.?" In a voice louder than it needed to be.

"No, Ma'am. Just moving in."

"Well, to make a long story short, the Journal is reporting that there are over 5,000 untested rape kits in the Albuquerque Police Department Crime Lab, some of which have been there for years. What the fuck?!? How does that happen?"

Rawlings took a deep breath. He didn't know the mayor well. Cheryl Romero had been a long-time member of the Albuquerque City Council, had been appointed Deputy Mayor three years before, and then had taken over when her predecessor had died of pancreatic cancer. She had won election in her own right for a full term two years before. By all accounts, a no nonsense, pragmatic, get it done politico.

The news took J.D. by surprise but he now understood why his wife was calling him. She'd obviously seen the article.

Mayor Romero said she would be calling a press conference that afternoon and wanted him and the Albuquerque Police Chief there as well.

"It's going to be a shit show and I need all the help I can get. See what you can find out between now and then." She hung up.

He hit line one.

Margaret Espinoza was no stranger to profanity given her years in the department. She rarely used it herself except for rare occasions of which this was one.

"There are 5,000 plus rape kits in the Crime Lab that have never been investigated. What the fuck!"

"Good mornin' to you, darling." She ignored him.

"I have a call into the Chief as should you. Darling."

"The mayor is having a press conference this afternoon and wants me and Chief Johnson there as well. Guessing she'll want him to do most of the talking."

"Better have a story to tell but I can't imagine what it is. Keep me posted, J.D. This is bad."

An hour later, he was on a Zoom call with the Mayor and Chief Johnson.

Ralph Johnson had taken over as Chief just six months before when the longtime Chief had tired of the politics and the bad publicity surrounding the department and had abruptly retired. Johnson had been Deputy Chief of the Las Vegas Department and had been hastily recruited and hired. It was a decision he regretted as soon as he opened the Journal that morning.

"Chief, how could this happen?"

There was a long pause.

"As best as I can tell, Your Honor, it is simply a question of manpower. We don't have the resources."

J.D. winced at his use of 'manpower.'

"We don't have enough people in the Department to do the work and we don't have enough District Attorneys to prosecute the perps even if we had the lab technicians to analyze the kits."

J.D. had to agree with the lack of assistant attorneys to prosecute 5,000 cases but in the years he had been with the office, this was the first he had heard of the backlog.

"Chief, the one thing we don't want to do is blame each other but this is the first I've heard of this. You're right. We don't have near enough assistants to make a dent in this, but it would have been nice to know about it."

Johnson thought for a moment.

"The problem is going to be that so many of these cases are too cold to prosecute. Victims will be impossible to locate, the time to prosecute the perps may have long passed, the witnesses are long gone as well. The logistics are a nightmare."

J.D. thought to himself that at least the chain of custody wasn't an issue because all 5,000 kits had been in the same place the entire time but that wasn't going to be a comfort to anybody.

The Mayor. "So, what do we say at the press conference this afternoon."

Chief Johnson. "The truth. The Department screwed up."

The Mayor. "What's the fix?"

"Manpower." J.D. winced again at the Chief's choice of words. "And money. We'll need to add a bunch of lab technicians to do the analyses of the kits, we'll need investigators to conduct field interviews, victim assistance programs, and we'll need a big team of lawyers to prosecute the cases that are viable." He paused. "And, as you know, we are running in the red more this year than last. We don't have the money."

J.D. "We'll have to go outside Albuquerque to get the money whether it's grants from the Justice Department or other programs around the country. We can't be the only city in the country with this kind of problem."

"So, here's what we'll do, gentlemen. We call the press conference for 3:00 PM in the auditorium at the city. I'll lead off, introduce both of you, have the Chief explain how it got to this point, and end with J.D. talking about potential funding sources and what needs to be done to clear up the backlog. And wear your dress blues. Signing off."

J.D. signed off and called his wife to fill her in. Unfortunately, she was at the scene of a multiple homicide in the Heights with little time to talk.

"Only advice I can give you when it comes to your time to talk, don't use the phrase 'manpower.' They'll kill you. Love you and good luck."

Chapter Two

Press Conference

At promptly 3:00 PM, Mayor Romero, Chief Johnson and District Attorney J.D. Rawlings walked into the packed City auditorium. Johnson had indeed dressed in his dress blues and J.D. had gone home and put on the best suit he had.

The Mayor opened the press conference by thanking the *Albuquerque Journal* for breaking the story, indicating that all hands were on deck to determine how the backlog had occurred, and, more importantly, how it could be fixed. She introduced Chief Johnson who stepped up to the podium and cleared his throat. J.D. hoped to God he wouldn't say 'manpower.'

"As best as we can tell, this backlog of uninvestigated rape kit cases has been the result of a lack of manpower over the past several years in all levels of the Police Department from lab technicians to victims' rights investigators to sexual assault officers. And a lack of assistant district attorneys to prosecute the cases."

J.D. winced at 'manpower' and then got irritated with the Chief's comment about the lack of attorneys to prosecute cases his office knew nothing about.

The Chief went on. "The issue has always been that the Department does not have enough money to fund the resources we need in those areas and, as many of you know, we are projected to run at a deficit for the coming year and we're just getting started. We will do everything we can and will transfer resources to the backlog issue but unfortunately that will leave other important functions of the Department with less to do more.

District Attorney Rawlings will address the 'manpower' issue from his office and then we'll take questions."

J.D. rose to the podium.

"Thank you, Chief. As Chief Johnson indicated, this is as much a question of money to fund the resources necessary as anything. We are not the only city in the country with this problem of a back log of rape kit investigations and we are already addressing and identifying funding sources from federal, state and private agencies and foundations. If we can get commitments of funding, we can begin the long process of identifying and investigating the cases.

Make no mistake, however, with this many cases over this many years, many of them will be 'cold cases' with victims and witnesses no longer available or unwilling to help and rapists difficult to find and prosecute even if we can match up DNA from the kits.

We're happy to take questions."

Dozens of hands shot up and the press conference went on for another two hours of some very hostile questioning mostly of Chief Johnson who on more than one occasion was called out on his use of 'manpower.'

"Chief," one reporter asked, "is the lack of 'manpower' simply the Department's way of saying this is just about women being attacked? If 5,000 men had been anally raped, would there be a backlog or would there have been enough 'manpower' to solve the problem?"

'Ouch.' J.D. thought to himself.

The conference finally ended a little before 6 with more questions posed than answers given and with the assurance by the Mayor in closing that the City would do everything in its power to break the logjam.

The Mayor, Vice Mayor, Chief and Deputy Chief, and J.D. met for a short time after the conference to debrief but it was blessedly short if for no other reason than there was little to debrief on. Albuquerque had a huge problem on its hands.

On the way home, J.D. got a text from Margaret saying she was still at the homicide scene but would be home shortly. J.D. didn't wait. He walked in the door, walked right to the freezer, pulled out the Tito's, poured himself a martini without the need for vermouth, and headed for the couch.

Margaret walked in ten minutes later, walked right to the freezer, pulled out the Tito's, poured herself a martini without the need for vermouth, and headed for the couch.

"So…how was your day?"

Chapter Three

The Beginning

Six weeks after the initial press conference, the Albuquerque Police Department received a grant from the federally funded Sexual Assault Kit Initiative Program of $2.4 million dollars to implement the steps necessary to undertake the laborious, tedious process of analyzing the kits. Lab technicians from independent agencies were hired and trained to do the hands-on work. Chief Johnson transferred several officers from other departments to the Sexual Assault Division to investigate and hopefully arrest those rapists who could be identified and found.

In partnership with the YWCA Domestic Crisis Center, money from the grant was used to train victims' assistance specialists to help those women who were identified and still needed services to help with the trauma of being raped.

J.D. assigned three of his assistants to work at least initially part time to develop a plan to prosecute those alleged rapists who could be identified through DNA or by any other means. But if things began to heat up as everybody hoped, his office would never have enough staff to prosecute those men or women who needed prosecution.

One might ask 'what took so long' and it was a fair question for which there were no good answers. The only redeeming feature was that the Mayor, Chief of Police and District Attorney were all relatively new to their jobs and therefore got at least somewhat of a pass on how this horror had all come to be in the first place. At least the new leadership was doing something.

J.D. and Margaret talked about the shortage of prosecutors and what to do. The answer? They needed veteran trial lawyers from the private sector to give back, to donate their time to see that as many victims as possible got justice.

Chapter Four

The Gang of Four Plus One

Margaret Espinoza had a plan and in early March convened a confidential meeting at their house of a disparate but powerful group of women in the city. She begrudgingly invited her husband because, after all, he was the District Attorney and, in addition, invited Mayor Romero, Chief Judge of the Bernalillo District Court Alexandra Kennedy, and the best criminal defense lawyer in at least Albuquerque, if not the entire Southwest, Rita Alverson. For obvious reasons, there were to be no notes and no mention of the meeting. The sole agenda item was how to staff an elite prosecutorial team from the private sector to see justice done.

Margaret knew that if business was to be done, it had to be before second drinks were handed out and so it was. The first thing was to establish criteria which consisted of lawyers who, in civil or criminal law, had tried cases. When so few cases were tried either civilly or criminally, it was a task not easily solved. A second issue, especially from Alverson's perspective, was whether criminal defense lawyers would want to be special prosecutors if they had spent their careers defending criminals. But at least they could be asked. A third issue was supervision and training in criminal law and that would have to come from the District Attorney's office. J.D. thought the three individuals already involved would be the supervisory team to select the cases, train the lawyers, and pick the cases that had the best chance of conviction. Another issue was whether the group should only be women and fortunately that thought was voted down but not without some animated discussion on 'manpower.' And finally, they helped themselves to a second drink and began to name names.

By the end of the night, the Gang of Four Plus One had identified 75 men and women who had tried cases in both the criminal and civil courts and were of all ages and sexes.

At the top of Judge Kennedy's list was, Jackie LaPointe, and right behind her a woman from the same firm, Johnston & Blackwell, Rosalind McManus. Alex swore the others to secrecy on where those names came from because her husband, Will Bennett, was in the same firm and she wasn't sure he'd appreciate his wife naming two of the best lawyers in the firm to this elite but pro bono team.

The other secret over a nightcap was that this meeting was never to be mentioned and those in attendance were never to be identified. And so it was.

The next day, a letter went out from the District Attorney of Bernalillo County, J.D. Rawlings, to 75 lawyers asking them to volunteer their time for the Special Sexual Assault Strike Team (Margaret's idea on the name) to prosecute those individuals charged with sexual assault who would come out of the rape kit backlog.

He got 55 yeses, the first two of whom were Jackie LaPointe and Rosalind McManus. Those two were not surprising but what was surprising was that half of the responses were from male lawyers. This was not a gender issue. This was a justice issue, pure and simple.

Chapter Five

Will, Jackie and Rosalind

Will Bennett was in his late 50's and having the time of his life, having married the love of his life and having avoided being killed on two or three occasions since his move to New Mexico. He had practiced law in Western Michigan for years, fallen in love with Alex Kennedy, and after his daughter graduated from law school, had decided to move to New Mexico. Miracle of miracles, he had studied for and passed the New Mexico Bar Exam and had joined a litigation firm doing pretty much the same kind of work he had done in Michigan.

Sometime after arriving in the Land of Enchantment, he had the opportunity to be in on the ground floor of a new firm made up of some friends and colleagues, both litigators and business lawyers. They named the firm Johnston & Blackwell, PLC after two of the better known lawyers in Albuquerque for curb appeal and name recognition. It had survived the murders of several of its partners but had flourished, nevertheless. Will had had success in several trials in which he represented individuals who had been injured because of the negligence of others or, in some cases, estates of people who had been killed. The business side of the firm was also doing well, and the firm began to grow.

Will Bennett had known Jackie LaPointe since she was a techie with the Alexandria Virginia Police Force. He was in Virginia trying to figure out who had murdered his best friend and his best friend's wife and Jackie had overseen wiring him for a meeting with a 'person of interest' as Detective Robert Davidson of the Alexandria Police Department had called him. She was a quiet young woman, heavily tattooed and pierced and Will hadn't given her much thought after she had wired him up.

But he and Alex, who had been with Will in Virginia, had made an impression on her and some weeks after the murders were solved and Alex and Will had gone back to Albuquerque, Jackie LaPointe called Will and 24 hours later showed up at their door in Old Town. A foster child and victim of abuse as a child, she was a loner and, with no ties anywhere, had decided to load up her car with her precious few belongings and head west. She had remembered Will and remembered he was from Albuquerque and figured Albuquerque was as good a place as any to set up.

Will and Alex were both quite taken with her, and Will got her a job as a 'gopher' with his original firm. She then moved with him when Johnston & Blackwell was started, ran IT for a while and then became the Office Manager. Along the way, Jackie was saving up and lasering tattoos and removing piercings.

She enrolled at the University of New Mexico Law School and as soon as she graduated with honors was hired as an associate at Johnston & Blackwell. From the start and no surprise to anyone, she was a rock star, smart, intuitive with a work ethic second to none.

She also met Josephine Lucas, a second-year anesthesiology resident at UNM, at a chance encounter at a Starbuck's and fell in love. They were married and had just recently added a baby daughter, Antonia, to their family. They called her Noni. Once Josephine finished her residency, she had joined the anesthesia group at UNM.

Rosalind McManus was a Legal Services lawyer who had been in an educational program for public service lawyers to teach them trial skills. Judge Kennedy had been on the faculty and thought Rosalind was one of the best young lawyers she had ever me. She called Will from the program and told him about her. He cold called her after the program was over, and, after a first interview, offered her a position with the firm. She accepted. And quickly became a second rock star.

 Rosalind was a poster child for the Irish – curly, red hair ('I have never been able to do anything about it'), fair skin with freckles on her nose, and tough as they come. Some years ago, someone had commented that she look so much like her mother that, Deidre McManus, that they could have been sisters. Her mother had beamed even though she was fighting a losing battle against ovarian cancer and Rosalind had thought the person to be visually impaired.

The two of them were the future of Johnston & Blackwell.

The one thing he had promised both was that they had the freedom to make decisions about their careers consistent with their values even if it meant taking on difficult cases and, in some cases, working for free.

It was a promise that was about to come back to haunt him.

On an early Monday morning in March, Will, as usual, was the first one in the office this time just ahead of Morton Blackwell, managing partner of the firm, and he was getting the first pot of coffee going when Jackie and Rosalind walked into the kitchen and asked, once the coffee was done, if they could have a word with him. He should have known something was in the wind.

The three of them got situated in his office with cups of coffee. Jackie took the lead and told Will that she and Rosalind had volunteered for the Strike Team to volunteer to prosecute sex assault cases from the backlog. Will knew three things. Somehow his wife was involved in this; two, the firm had way too much work for Rosalind and Jackie to be doing what he knew would be time-consuming and grueling; and three, he respected them even more if that was possible for what they were doing.

"Are you asking me or telling me?"

Jackie: "A little of both."

"Done. Keep me posted and if I can help, keep me in the loop."

Almost in unison. "Love you, Boss."

Chapter Six

Bernalillo County District Attorney J.D. Rawlings

For the number of years that J.D. had been an Assistant District Attorney, he had worked hard and had won the praise of his superiors for his talent, work ethic and success in the courtrooms of the county.

Why in the world he ever thought it would be a good idea to run for election to be the District Attorney was beyond him, and that night after he got home from the press conference, he wondered aloud to Margaret whether he could push a 'reset' button. They both knew the answer.

Now some weeks later working routinely 18 hours a day seven days a week, he wondered again what the hell he had been thinking. As the money from the grant was coming in, J.D., along with the ABQ Police, was hiring the independent lab technicians to help with the overwhelming task of testing 5,000 kits. Each test took up to 50 hours of painstaking work, so the time spent was beyond even worrying about.

He was reminded of the book by Anne Lamott Bird by Bird in which you just put your head down and worked on a bird until it was done and when it was done, you started on the next one. He shared that with the lab technicians and his own staff with only mixed success. What did help was that J.D. was working as hard as they were if not harder and the men and women took that attitude to mean that if he could do it, so could they. So, they did.

As the test results were finished, they were sent off to the Combined DNA Index System (CODIS) which was an FBI support system set up to compare DNA samples on a national basis. Results were yet to come back.

It also didn't help that the media had made this a national issue. New Mexico still had thousands of untested rape kits.   There was plenty of blame to go around and media outlets incessantly talked about a lack of funding; a lack of technology; and a District Attorney's office that was ill prepared and understaffed to handle the cases even if they had been tested.

A bright spot was the list of private attorneys that the Gang of Four Plus One had put together and the overwhelming affirmative response they had gotten back.

The first training for the group was set for the coming Saturday and J.D. marshalled his group of lab technicians, sex division police officers, and the attorneys from his office who were now 100% dedicated to the investigation and prosecution of the offenders discovered from the test results.

J.D. had hoped to have at least the first training be confidential and to accomplish that got the Chief Judge of the 2nd Judicial District, Alexandra Kennedy, to have the session held in the ceremonial courtroom at the District Court. Additional security was added, and participation was by invitation only.

Rosalind and Jackie were two of the first to arrive.

Chapter Seven

Thank You

Judge Kennedy opened the training by thanking all of those in attendance for their willingness to help with the monstrous task ahead of them and committing the court's resources to help in whatever way it could. She turned the program over to J.D. to introduce the day.

"Good morning and let me echo Judge Kennedy's remarks about how grateful we are that you are willing to help. You are a huge part of getting our hands around this difficult, complex situation.

"I could spend a lot of time talking about how we got here but, frankly, that doesn't do us much good. What we need to do is focus on the future and what all of us can do.

"That having been said, let me give you some staggering and disheartening figures. 73% of the backlog is from Albuquerque and the rest are scattered throughout the counties. We are coordinating with the sheriffs in each of the counties to have their untested kits sent to us as the central repository for the state.

 "A news article recently suggested that 20% of the kits were not tested because the police did not find the victims 'credible.' Another 20%+ were not tested either because of a lack of contact with the victim or lack of cooperation.

"Think about that, ladies and gentlemen, if that's true, over 40% of the victims took the time to go to a health care facility to go through the emotional toll of being tested and we either didn't believe them or couldn't find them. That is outrageous.

"That has changed and, from here on out, there is follow-up for every person who has been attacked and who has completed the testing.

"The answer to this problem is twofold. One, additional resources of which all of you are a major addition. As you know, we have received a grant of $2.5 million dollars and we are using that money as it comes in to add lab technicians and increase the Sexual Assault Division of the Police Department. We are adding Assistant District Attorneys who will join our existing group in prosecuting cases. But given the backlog we are a drop in the bucket which is why we need you. You are the other solution."

"We are working with the Albuquerque YWCA Domestic Abuse Center to increase victim outreach to make sure the victims, male or female, are given the resources necessary to recover from the physical and emotional trauma of the attacks. And to make sure we track those victims moving forward."

"Certainly, there are obstacles to overcome. Statute of limitations issues on second, third- and fourth-degree felonies, finding victims after many years, and finding potential defendants are all issues. So, we won't win them all but it sure as hell won't be for lack of trying.

"I've talked too long and there is much to go over. You will learn about the actual testing of the kits; the degrees of sexual assault and how to distinguish how to charge; the supervision of the cases that we decide to charge; the victim outreach initiative that I just touched on; the reporting of our results to CODIS which is the national FBI DNA support program where all of our results so far are being sent and those in the future as well."

He stopped for a moment and was afraid he was going to be overcome with emotion. In front of him were 50 plus lawyers all of whom were successful trial lawyers who were willing to help bring justice to victims of sexual assault they didn't even know existed. He took a deep breath and paused for a second.

"Let me introduce two individuals to you. Alice Robbins is an Assistant District Attorney who has volunteered to lead the prosecutors in our office do whatever we can to help. And Mary Elizabeth Connery, Chief of the Albuquerque Police Department Crime Lab, who will take you through the intricacies from receipt of the test from the hospital or clinic to reporting out the results to CODIS. Mary Elizabeth?"

For the next several hours the lawyers learned about the process from when a report of a sexual assault is originally made to the initial investigation of the scene to getting the victim immediate help to getting the victim to the health care facility to check for injuries and to complete the rape kit to testing for DNA to further investigation and ultimately charging and pretrial discovery to either a plea or a trial.

It was a lot to take in but there were no dummies in this group.

For Jackie LaPointe, first and foremost in her mind was Leslie Helm whose kit was one of the 5,000 sitting on a shelf in the crime lab. She had an obsessive desire to get justice for Leslie.

At the end of the training, Judge Kennedy asked each of them to stand and raise their right hands to take an oath as Special Assistant District Attorneys. The Special Sexual Assault Strike Team was now officially in place.

Chapter Eight

First Case

The next Wednesday Rosalind and Jackie got an email from Alice Robbins who had been introduced as the head of the three-person assistant district attorneys in charge of prosecuting sexual assault cases, asking them to meet her at their earliest convenience.

"Jackie, whaddaya have this afternoon?"

"Nothing that can't wait." She smiled. "Just don't tell Will."

Rosalind emailed Robbins back and asked if that afternoon was soon enough. Turned out it was.

At 3 that afternoon, they were ushered into a conference room in the Schiff Office Building. A couple of minutes later they were joined by a woman about their age who introduced herself as Alice Robbins. Neither Rosalind nor Jackie knew what to expect having only seen her from a distance at the orientation but, whatever it was, Robbins didn't fit the picture of a tough, no-nonsense prosecutor. Thin and in shape, neck length blonde hair, a face that could have been a model, and clothes that didn't come off the rack, she exuded warmth and kindness. As time went on, though, they would soon learn that Alice Robbins had the heart and courage of a lion. They would also learn that Alice Robbins was obsessed with her job and obsessed with finding justice for the victims, an obsession that it seemed to Jackie and Rosalind bordered on irrationality.

Just as she asked them to sit down, they were joined by J.D. Rawlings. Both had met him but were surprised the District Attorney himself was taking the time to join the meeting.

"Before I turn the meeting over to Alice, I need a promise from the two of you."

They nodded.

"Promise me that you will never tell Will Bennett his wife is the one who insisted you be invited to be members of the Strike Team, OK?"

They nodded again.

"Alice."

For the next 45 minutes, they were briefed on a case that had cleared the backlog in the lab. DNA results from the test were sent to CODIS and had identified a possible match with a man that matched the physical description of a man involved in a sexual assault three years before in a house in Albuquerque. His name was Jerry Kent and his DNA had first been picked up six years ago in a burglary. There had been a couple of other hits but small-time stuff like robbery and burglary but no sex and no violence and only jail time. There was a warrant out for his arrest.

The victim, who was using an alias Mary Smith, had been home getting ready to go to her job at Whole Foods. She shared a house with several roommates all of whom were already at work. She answered a knock at the door and a man pushed his way into the hallway holding a knife and telling her to keep quiet or she would be dead. He wore a ski mask and gloves and spoke with a slight Hispanic accent.

Jackie felt a chill of recognition at the description. It was exactly what had happened to Leslie Helm.

He had ordered Mary to take her clothes off and pushed her onto the couch with the knife at her throat. He tried to insert his penis but ejaculated on her pubic area instead. He went ahead and got his penis into her vagina, pulled out almost immediately, stood up, dressed and, without a word, left the house.

Mary's first thought was to wash herself off but instead called her best friend who told her to call the police and report the attack. She did, was interviewed at the house by a male uniformed officer, who then turned her over to a woman officer who took her to the hospital. The nurse in the ER performed a vaginal exam and told Mary she would be advised if the investigation turned anything up.

Like so many other victims, she never heard from the police again.

In the three years since the attack, Mary Smith had gotten on with her life as best as she could. Other than her friend who she had called, she never told anyone about the attack, not her family, not her friends, and not her boyfriend at the time. That relationship hadn't lasted long after the attack and there had been a series of relationships since then all of which had ended because of her unwillingness or inability to be intimate. It had not helped that she had gained 50 pounds, quit exercising, and, in her own words, had become a 'couch potato.' She now lived alone.

Alice Robbins had contacted Mary Smith to tell her that they had a DNA lead on her attacker and that she wanted two members of the Strike Team to meet with her. She had most reluctantly agreed.

If the two attorneys were interested in the case, Alice would set up a meeting with Mary and the two of them. Both Rosalind and Jackie agreed without question.

As the meeting was winding down, Jackie told Alice and J.D. about her friend Leslie and how similar it seemed to this one. Alice shook her head.

"Possible, Jackie, but unlikely. This is such a common M.O. for these assholes. Ski mask, gloves, knife, threats of death. What is also common is that very few of them wear condoms. Too much trouble because it might take two hands? We think it's because they think it's macho to leave their stench on their victims." Alice paused. "But you never know. Give me your friend's name and the date of the assault and I'll check on it. I'll call Mary and see if we can set something up. Do you two work on weekends?"

They both laughed. "What's a weekend?"

On the way out of the conference room, Rosalind turned.

"Jerry Kent doesn't sound very Hispanic to me."

"It isn't," J.D. said, "but 90% of the gringos in violent sex cases use a ski mask and a Hispanic accent. Not too hard to say 'shut up or you're dead' with an accent."

They nodded, said goodbye and left. And stopped to get a drink on the way back to the office too excited about their first assignment to go right back to work. Just as long as Will didn't find out about his wife.

Chapter Nine

Mary Smith

Saturday morning at 9, armed with a description of what Mary looked like, Jackie and Rosalind met her at Peet's Coffee and Tea Shop on Alameda. She was in a booth by herself, heavy, and wrapped in a scarf of some sort she kept up close to her face, a baseball cap down over eyes, and dark sunglasses that covered most of her face.

They introduced themselves and got to the point in short order. No reason to exchange pleasantries. They confirmed that the DNA from the rape kit matched a small-time crook and that there was currently a warrant out for his arrest that included the attack on her three years ago.

"What do you want from me? It's been three years. Look at me. Does it look like I need to relive what happened? Don't you think I relive it every day? No friends, no boyfriends, fifty pounds heavier than I was. Why would I do it to myself?"

"Closure? Knowing you got justice for what he did to you?"

"Justice." It was almost a snarl. "Justice would have been if it'd never happened in the first place. But it did. And there will never be justice. What does he get if he's guilty? Few years in prison, maybe less. Time for good behavior? You shitting me?"

"With the DNA match, we can limit what we'll need from you, Mary," Rosalind started. "You can't identify him, the Hispanic accent was probably fake, and he wore a mask and gloves. The main thing is he broke into your house, held you at knife point and raped you without your consent."

"So why bother me if you don't need much from me?"

"Because we want you to know we have a match and have the go ahead from the D.A.'s office to go after the guy. We just wanted you to know."

"What if he pleads and goes to jail, gets out, remembers the house, and somehow tracks me down? This time he'd kill me. Although not sure that's much worse than my life now."

She stood up as suddenly as her weight would permit.

"It was nice meeting you and thanks for doing this but don't on my account." She left the shop, got into a nondescript car of some years past and left.

"Well, for our first interview, that went well, Jackie. Plaintiffs in our civil practice are a lot more forthcoming. What do we do different?"

Jackie thought for a moment. "You know what we need is some time with women – and men – who have been raped. You and I need to have a better understanding of what happens in the aftermath when they get involved in the criminal justice system. The one thing I've always heard is that the victim gets cross examined like it was their fault, like they really wanted it, like they dressed in a way to attract men, etc., etc."

Rosalind paused to think about what she said next. "You've told me a lot about what you went through growing up, Jackie. Why is this so different?"

It was Jackie's turn to pause. "I don't know why I'm different or even if I am. I know what happened to me is somewhere in a locked box in my mind and I've lost the combination. Josephine would be better explaining me than me and probably you better explaining me than me. And just maybe being a member of the Strike Team is little bit of that box leaking out."

"And you, what about you, Ms. Save the World? Why you?"

"Because I am the result of a rape that occurred 31 years ago when my mom was 16 years old. Son of the biggest car dealer in town, captain of the football team, Homecoming King, Big Man on Campus. Asked my mom for a date, got her in the back seat of his daddy's Cadillac, and raped her. When she realized she was pregnant, my mom's parents sent her away to have the baby. Abortion for them was out of the question. 'Course it shouldn't have been their decision, but it was and here I am."

It was news to Jackie. "What happened to the bio dad? "

"Grew up to take over the car dealership, ran it into bankruptcy either through what he was putting up his nose or down his throat, killed himself by driving a brand-new Cadillac off a cliff. Left a wife and two young children. Manly thing to do."

"His family?"

"No idea. And don't care."

"Will know any of this?"

"I don't think so. When I first came to Albuquerque, Alex and Will asked a few questions but not a lot. Nice thing about New Mexico, I think. Doesn't matter where you're from but who you are now. Why I love it here."

"Wonder if Will understands who he's got on his hands?" Rosalind smiled.

"Well, if he didn't, being married to Judge Kennedy has been an education."

Jackie's turn to smile. "You think?"

"So, where do we go from here?"

"Tell Alice what happened, see if we can meet with some survivors, and go from here."

They toasted the last of their coffee cups and left, Jackie home to be with Josephine and Noni and Rosalind back to the office to catch up.

Chapter Ten

Survivors

On Monday morning, they reported back to Alice Robbins at the D.A.'s office and filled her in on the less than stellar interview with Mary Smith.

"Alice, we got to talking Saturday after we met with Mary. I'm a survivor of sexual assault and Rosalind is the product of another one. In our lives, we have met any number of women – and some men – who have been victims and some we've gotten to know well enough to hear their stories.

But the one thing we weren't prepared for is how, as prosecutors, we interview them to give them a comfort level that we're on their side, that they don't need to be afraid of us, that they don't need to be afraid of the system. I don't know about Rosalind, but where I thought we really fucked up was when she said that when he gets out – or gets acquitted – he'll track her down and kill her this time. We had no answer for that even if there is one. We think the Strike Team needs to know how to handle those reactions.

J.D. talked about 20% of the victims being noncooperative and another 20% the cops don't find credible. So, 40% of the victims we interview if there's a match is problematic."

For Jackie, as long a speech as she had made outside the courtroom probably in her life.

Alice looked at both for a long time without saying anything. To the point where both Jackie and Rosalind got a little uncomfortable. Finally.

"The reason I went to law school and took this job is because I was gang raped by football players at Colorado State when I was a freshman. I swore then that I would make this my life's goal to put as many of these assholes away for as long as I could. And here I am. And here I'll stay to catch everyone of these sons of bitches who do this to us." They both heard the anger and the bitterness.

"I've interviewed dozens of women and children who have been assaulted. With all that experience, I can't give you a textbook on how to do it. And I've fucked up dozens of interviews because I didn't do it right.

"What if we put together a focus group of survivors and did a tutorial on interviewing victims not when the assault occurs or at the hospital when the test is being done but when victims are faced with the criminal justice system and the hurdles they'll face? For example, 'blame the victim.' Number One defense theory and theme in every rape case I've ever handled. Much can be done to get victims ready if the case goes to trial but the vics need to know that's on the radar from the get-go."

"Include the prosecutors?" Jackie.

"I don't think we should for the first one, just the survivors. Prosecutors will be defensive and try to lead the discussion. We need to hear from just the victims and what they need from us. Rosalind?"

Rosalind thought about it for a minute. "Agree we keep it to victims for the first session."

We videotape it and then have each member of the Strike Team view it." Alice Robbins warmed to the topic. "Nope, include mandatory viewing of every prosecutor in the state who handles sexual assault cases. We'll loan it to the Federal Defender's office and to the tribal prosecutors. Voluntary for them but who is going to say it's a bad idea?"

She was almost out of breath. "OK, you two. If there's nothing else, I need to get to work. Probably ought to let J.D. know, don'cha think?" She winked and stood up. "No reason some of that grant money doesn't help all of us."

On their way out of the conference room, Alice stopped them.

"Oh. Forgot to mention, cops have an address for Jerry Kent, the perp for Mary. Probably try to pick him up today. 'Bye."

Chapter Eleven

Jerry Kent

As Chief of the Homicide Division of the Albuquerque Police Department, Margaret Espinoza would get a daily print out of any deaths other than natural causes to decide whether her division should get involved in a potential homicide investigation.

That Monday morning, Margaret was reviewing the daily sheet and noted that police officers had tried to serve an arrest warrant on a Jerry Kent for several crimes including a sexual assault that had occurred three years before. The officers had announced their presence at an apartment that had seen better days in the South Valley and when there was no response had asked the manager of the apartments to let them in.

They had found the body of Jerry Kent on his couch with a .22 caliber pistol in his left hand and a gunshot wound to his left temple. Even with the naked eye, the officers could see gun powder around the entrance wound.

Not surprisingly in the area where he lived, no one had heard a gunshot or, as was more likely, the neighbors heard so many gunshots, this one didn't stand out.

The Sergeant called to the scene by the uniformed officers came to the logical conclusion that Kent had, for whatever reason, killed himself. There was no note or anything else to indicate suicide, but the Sergeant could come to no other conclusion. The only thing that was odd about the suicide was that Jerry Kent had no idea there was a warrant out for his arrest. So why now?

The medical examiner was called, examined the body, and agreed it was suicide. Case closed.

To Espinosa, there was no reason to disagree with the Sergeant's conclusion and the M.E.'s conclusion and she moved on down the printout. The report on the gun came back and its serial numbers had been filed off. Unidentifiable.

Except that Jerry Kent was right-handed and that caught Espinoza's attention. Some months before, she had been involved in a "murder-suicide" investigation in which the wife had shot her husband and then killed herself. Except that the gun was in the wife's right hand and she was left handed. Only weeks later had that mystery been solved when the son of the parents confessed to killing them both. Here, it was the other way around.

By that Monday afternoon, the D.A.'s office was notified of the death, Alice Robbins called Rosalind and Jackie to give them the news and they, in turn, got hold of Mary Smith to tell her.

Case closed...except that Espinoza kept a copy of the printout in her "To Be Saved" folder in her desk. For her, the parts didn't quite fit.

Chapter Twelve

Victims

Two weeks later on a Wednesday evening, six victims of sexual assault, five women and one man, agreed to be interviewed by Alice Robbins, Rosalind McManus, and Jackie LaPointe. It was done by Zoom and the faces of the victims were blurred and the names anonymous.

The question asked of all of them was simple. After the initial assault, rape testing, and investigation, what did they need from the legal system up to and through trial?

The answers were uniform and, to the three lawyers, stunning.

All of them wanted to be a part of the process and to be kept up to date on the progress, the investigation, the initial arrest, the arraignment and the run up to trial. For the trial, they unanimously agreed they wanted help to prepare to meet their attackers face to face. If legally possible, they wanted help preparing their testimony, and wanted help with the dangers of cross examination from being accused of being the consenting party to the assault, to wrongly identifying the perpetrator, to having their backgrounds or past sexual history used against them for starters.

The lesson learned that night was the victim wanted to be part of the prosecutorial team.

And upon conviction, they wanted their say in the sentencing phase.

It was an emotional meeting and one that had Rosalind and Jackie in tears at one point or another. Alice Robbins seemed completely devoid of emotion and both Rosalind and Jackie thought it was because she had seen and heard it all in her career.

At the end of the session, Alice thanked them all for their help and promised that their ideas had been heard and would be incorporated into the process from here on out.

Just before the session ended, one participant who had said very little said, "More than anything, we don't want to be forgotten. We want justice for what they did to us."

The three lawyers sat around after the Zoom ended.

Robbins spoke first. "We could do a protocol that periodically contacted the victim and told them where we were in the process even if there hadn't been any progress. A lot of the vics may know the perps and could bring us up to date on what they heard.

"And for trial prep, we could do video on direct examination and possible topics for cross examination, take them to the courthouse, show them the witness chair, maybe even have them go over the jury questionnaires to help us identify potential good ones and bad ones. The obstacle is to make sure that if we help with witness preparation, the defense doesn't to cross examine the victims that they were helped with their testimony by the prosecutors."

Jackie thought that would be a real tight rope for a defense lawyer for an alleged rapist to cross examine a victim because they had been helped by the lawyers for the people but it was something to consider and she kept quiet.

They got up to leave the conference room with wishes for happy holidays.

Rosalind and Jackie hugged each other goodbye.

"Too bad we have day jobs."

"See you at the shop."

Chapter Thirteen

Progress

Like any story, the story about the untested rape kits faded to old news in the media as other stories competed for their 15 minutes of fame.

One of them brought Detective Jorge Rodriguez into his boss's office one morning barely able to stifle laughter that was close to hysterical. Detective Rodriguez had been a Sergeant with APD and had gotten to know Margaret Espinoza at dozens of homicide scenes over the years. She had been so impressed by him that when she was promoted to Chief of the Homicide Division, she pulled some strings, got Jorge a promotion, and appointed him second in command of the Division. There had been a little grumbling from some of the other members of the Division, but it soon died down. They too had been at too many homicide scenes with Rodriguez and knew how good he was.

He knocked and Margaret told him to come in.

"This will hit the news tonight and the Journal tomorrow, but I have to tell you. We just arrested a woman who, while her husband was asleep on the couch, lit him on fire. It woke him up and he went running out of the house to put himself out only to have his wife run over him eight times with her van. One of the neighbors called 911 and when the officers got there, she told them she was trying to put the fire out."

He paused and then convulsed in laughter which caused Margaret to join him for several seconds while all the while the detectives in the squad room wondered what the hell was so funny.

Tears streaming down his cheeks by this time, Jorge caught his breath and said, "You just can't make this shit up, Chief."

Margaret also stopped long enough to ask what the hell the case was doing in homicide.

"Why aren't they gonna charge her with arson and leave us out of it?" Which set off another round of laughter.

Jorge finally responded, "Well, running him over eight times in fact put the fire out. Unfortunately, it wasn't the fire that killed him."

She shook her head. Working homicide was always a tension between the barbarism and stupidity of humanity and its goodness. Some days were easier than others.

"Thanks, Jorge. This may be the brightest part of my day." When he left, she called her husband, J.D. Rawlings, and told him what was coming his way.

"Eight times? She ran over him eight times? Seems like a garden hose would have worked a little better. Jesus. See you tonight, hon."

"Thought I'd brighten your day, babe."

Rawlings turned back to the report on his desk that described the progress the APD and his office and the crime lab were making in the months they'd been working on the rape kits.

The lab had started with the oldest which went back 17 years and the newest which was a week old. The technicians had gotten through the first 400 of the oldest kits but they were the easy ones. Most were barred from prosecution because they were too old in terms of time because of the facts of the case as the prosecutors understood them, twelve were criminal sexual conduct in the first degree for which there was no time limit to bring charges. The new ones were taking more time.

The Mary Smith/Jerry Kent case had been an anomaly because the DNA from some of his prior crimes had cross matched to be a fit. Otherwise, it was a bit like 'looking for a needle in a haystack.' In Rawlings' mind, the whole project needed to go faster.

What was particularly infuriating to him was that the percentage of 'don't believe the victim' or 'can't find the victim' was significantly higher in the more recent cases. To Rawlings, that was an issue laid clearly at the feet of the Albuquerque Police Department under its prior leadership at all levels and a conversation he and Chief Johnson were having on an ongoing basis.

There was a knock at his door and Julie Stahl stuck her head in. "Mayor Romero on 1."

"Thanks, Julie." He took a deep breath and picked up the phone.

"Good morning, Your Honor."

"I've decided we've known each other long enough to be 'Cheryl' and 'J.D.' You OK with that?"

"Perfect, Your...Cheryl."

"Better. Here's my cell phone number you can call day or night," and she ran off a number with a 616 area code.

J.D. wrote it down and gave her his number, one that was shared by very few. "616. Where's that?"

"Grand Rapids, Michigan. Grew up in West Michigan in the summertime, daughter of migrant workers who every year traveled to Michigan from Mexico to pick blueberries. That's where I got the phone. From the start, I wanted to get into politics, but it wasn't the friendliest place for a Hispanic woman so I moved to Albuquerque several years ago. Seemed a better fit." No mistaking the sarcasm.

"But that's not why I'm calling. Turns out there is something like 'Traveling Nurses' for lab technicians. Called in a chit with a friend at the Felipe Ruiz Foundation and he gave us a grant for $250,000. Not exactly in keeping with the mission of the Foundation but sexually assaulting women was damn close."

J.D. thought for a minute. The Foundation had been set up in the name of Felipe Ruiz who had died in a cave in at a construction site. J.D.'s good friend, Will Bennett, had sued the construction company where Felipe had worked and, against all odds, had gotten a verdict for $18,000,000. A lot of the money had gone into a Foundation to help disadvantaged youth in the Albuquerque area. It had plenty of business.

The mayor went on. "So I got hold of the company that does both nurses and lab technicians, told them I would double what they were being paid now and was told there were 5 technicians in Detroit I should call. Gave me the number of one of them, called, offered them a 6-month gig, and 15 minutes later, she called back and said all of them were in. Day after tomorrow, they arrive in Albuquerque on Southwest at 9:45 AM direct from Detroit. Have Mary Elizabeth or her deputy meet them and get them to the lab. We'll decide on where they'll stay."

"How is she ever supposed to recognize them, Cheryl?"

"Thought of that, J.D. They'll all be wearing white lab coats."

"Anybody mention this to the chief of the lab in Detroit?"

Pause. "Better to be forgiven than ask for permission, J.D. I'll get around to it...day after tomorrow once I know they're here." The phone went dead.

He stared at the phone for a minute. And then smiled. 'Woman's got stones.' And went back to the report.

Chapter Fourteen

Nightmare on Central

That night, Jackie LaPointe left the Johnson & Blackwell office on Central and 5th at 10 PM and began the two block walk to the parking lot. Downtown Albuquerque had tried to reimagine itself any number of times over the last several years and while progress had been made, it was still sketchy with too many bars and too many drunks and too many homeless and not enough people committed to living downtown. The firm had taken over a beautiful, well-appointed space from a now defunct law firm, and it was a pearl for the downtown area. Except that it was on the second floor of a 19th century building and all but invisible to anybody unless they were looking for it.

She was a block away from the lot walking past an alley when an arm reached out, grabbed her, and pulled her into the alley. There were three of them and they wore Halloween masks, hoodies and jeans. She was pulled farther into the alley, and one began to tear at the suit jacket she was wearing. Another held his hand over her mouth and had a knife at her throat. Jackie was pulled to the ground on her knees as they continued to tear at her clothes. She noticed all three wore expensive athletic shoes. Not homeless these men. She smelled the alcohol and realized where their courage had come from.

Thus began a series of very bad decisions for the men. First, none of them realized that being assaulted by three men in a dark alley was nothing compared to what

Jackie LaPointe had been through in her life and therefore fear was an absent emotion. Second, none of them wore gloves and their DNA was going to be all over Jackie whether she survived or not. Third, they didn't realize she was a member of the Sexual Assault Strike Team and was well aware of the importance of gathering the DNA. And finally, and far most importantly, they didn't realize that Jackie always carried a six-inch knife in a sheath on her right ankle. From her position on her hands and knees and with the men more interested in her clothes and her body, the subtle movement to retrieve the knife went unnoticed.

The first victim was the man holding the knife in one hand and his other over her mouth. With all the strength she could muster, she drove the knife upward directly into the center of the man's jeans and buried it to the hilt; her second move was to pull forward on the knife before pulling it out doing as much damage as she could to his scrotum, penis, and surrounding tissue.

There was a high pitched, almost feminine scream as the man dropped his knife and fell backwards dislodging the Donald Trump mask and revealing a white twenty something male grabbing what was left of his scrotum. He continued to scream.

A fifth mistake for the other two was that, not knowing what had happened to President Trump, they were paralyzed where they stood which made the first Clown's Achilles heels easy targets for Jackie's knife. She got them both and when he tried to turn and run, his feet simply didn't obey, and he collapsed on the ground. His friend was still screaming at that same high pitch from a few seconds ago.

The third man, realizing that things were not going exactly as planned, turned to run but, by this time, Jackie had gotten to her feet and a step later, had driven the knife deep into the right side of the man's lower back and had yanked to the right until the knife cleared. His Clown mask around his neck, he ran from the alley clutching his side.

She called 911 and calmly described what had happened and where she was.

Despite anecdotal evidence that it took hours for the ABQ Police to respond to 911 calls, two patrol cars were at the head of the alley within seconds and 4 officers with guns drawn approached the scene. They took in the scene of a disheveled but intact Jackie LaPointe holding a very big knife, a white male lying on the ground whispering 'fuck, fuck, fuck' and another white male on the ground holding his crotch and now into a whimpering phase.

"Ma'am, we probably ought to hold the knife."

Jackie turned it over to the officer, introduced herself, and told the officers what had happened. She described the wounds to Trump and the Clown on the ground as well as the other Clown who, at best, was going to be at an urgent care center for the knife wound in his side.

"Jesus," said one of the other officers, "one will never walk right again and the other probably won't either but that's the least of his problems."

The police ordered up 'buses' for the two victims and Jackie asked that she be transported as well to get the DNA samples off her from the men's hands and from the blood that had speckled her pants. Two of the officers got her in the back of their patrol car and got her to the University of New Mexico Hospital ER where she underwent an evaluation including preserving her skin and blood spots with swabs. Jackie called Josephine, described very briefly what had happened, and said she'd be home soon. She also called Will Bennett with the same message who immediately insisted that he come down to the ER. She was about to object but knew him well enough to know it would be of no use.

While she was in one of the bays, she could hear gurneys being rolled into the ER, one with a victim who was still whimpering who she recognized as Trump and one who was moaning quietly who she assumed was one of the Clowns. She unnecessarily reminded the nurse about gathering their DNA.

The two officers said their goodbyes and left just as Will was coming through the doors.

Male officer to female officer. "Christ, you don't carry a knife in an ankle sheath, do you?"

She just smiled at him and walked to the patrol car.

Will talked himself past the triage nurse and got to the bay where Jackie was. He hugged her and tears ran down his cheeks.

"Boss, I'm OK. Really. It's OK."

He sat on the edge of the bed holding her hand, composed himself, make her call Alex herself to say she was all right, and then were interrupted by a woman who introduced herself as Lieutenant Sheila Jackson of the Albuquerque Police Department Sex Crimes Unit.

She took a statement from Jackie that had her go over the details and then got up to leave secretly smiling to herself that of all the terrible things she had to do as a part of her job, this night was a pretty good payback.

Just as she was leaving, she turned and pulled Jackie's knife out of her jacket to give back to her.

"We don't need this anymore. Thought you might be more comfortable with it." And left.

On her way back to the office, Jackson got a call that a young man named Beland had turned up at the Presbyterian Hospital Emergency Department with a serious knife wound to his right side and was being prepped for surgery. The Lieutenant allowed herself a small smile. Three for three.

Jackie got discharged and Will drove her to the parking lot. They drove past the alley on the way, and it was taped off with crime scene tape. They could see the crime investigation unit in the alley.

'Wonder if they'll find his balls?' He thought to himself and smiled the same smile Lieutenant Jackson had. 'Could have been awful. But tonight, it wasn't.'

Jackie drove home and hugged Josephine hard, then she and Josephine went in and sat with Noni for a long time. They came back out, she helped herself to a generous Jameson's and now, after midnight, crawled into bed. As she lay next to the love of her life who was snoring slightly, it was only then that the shock and the horror of what might have been sunk in. And she cried, not for herself, but for all the women for whom this night would have been at the very least a nightmare they would never wake up from or, worse, the last of their lives.

Chapter Fifteen

Aftermath

The next morning, Jackie got to the office early, made some coffee for herself and went to her office. When Rosalind arrived, Jackie filled her in. Rosalind was stoic but clearly shaken and had the same feeling as Jackie had had last night. Anybody but Jackie, including herself, and it would have turned out very differently.

At 10:00 AM, Will called her and asked her to join him in the conference room. He wasn't alone. In addition to Will, there was Alexandra Kennedy, Chief Judge of the Bernalillo County District Court; Margaret Espinoza, Chief of the Homicide Division for the Albuquerque Police Department; J.D. Rawlings, Bernalillo County District Attorney; Alice Robbins, head of the prosecutor's side of the Sexual Assault Strike Team; and Lieutenant Detective Sheila Jackson from last night. Rosalind McManus and Josephine Lucas were also there.

Josephine started. "You've been through a lot, my love, and there are going to be some hard times ahead. We all wanted to be here to tell you we've got your back and will do anything we can. We hope you will get some professional counseling as much as you hate it. Lots of resources."

Sheila Jackson went next. "We've identified the three men. Ricky Johnson aka Trump; Ben Wise aka the Clown; and Mark Beland aka the other Clown are all sophomores at the University of New Mexico. Frat boys, party animals, not likely to ever be juniors given their grade points." She looked at her notes. "Johnson will be in the hospital for several days and is currently in surgery. He has lost both testicles and his penis is very badly damaged. His injuries are permanent...to say the least. Wise will be operated on today or tomorrow for attempted repairs of complete lacerations of both of his Achilles tendons. Trouble for him is the lacerations are at the top of the tendon which makes surgery and recovery more difficult. He is young but unlikely ever to run or participate in any sports again. Beland is still in the hospital – the laceration to his side required removal of his right kidney that had been severed in two and several dozen staples both internally stitching the muscles back together and externally stitching the skin together. They want to keep him long enough to rule out infection."

She paused. "All of will be charged with several felonies and, assuming guilt by pleas or jury verdicts, they will spend several years in prison. DNA puts all three of them in the alley and on your person."

She paused again. "While the results are preliminary, all three DNA results place them at a gang rape several weeks ago at their fraternity house. Two of the three have DNA matches on a series of sexual assaults at or near the campus. We have started the process of contacting the victims."

Jackie. "I'd like to be a part of the prosecution team."

J.D. "Well, there's a surprise. But you can't be because you're a material witness in your own assault."

Rosalind. "I've already volunteered. I got your six, as the cops say, as well as the backs of all the victims."

Jackie smiled. "Copy that."

Jackson's phone buzzed and she excused herself. Back in a minute, she announced that Ricky Johnson had died on the operating table. The trauma team was never able to get the bleeding under control and he bled out.

Silence. No emotion by anybody. Especially Will thought it odd there wasn't more on Jackie's face – joy, grief, sadness. But there was nothing. What he didn't know was that this was not the first time Jackie had killed nor the second nor the third.

The group broke with hugs to Jackie and Josephine and dispersed.

Will to Rosalind and Jackie. "Any chances of getting some real work done today?"

That night, Will and Alex had a night to themselves along with Jinks, Jigs and LacyB. He poured them both a Jameson's, she started to heat up a Costco meal, and they settled back in the quiet of their   Old Town home. They caught up on Jackie. Alex had noticed the complete lack of emotion in her as well when the detective had told the group about Ricky Johnson. They came to the same conclusion they had always had – there was a history about Jackie LaPointe she would never share. Work for Alex was still herding the cats as the Chief Judge and cases, if they went to trial at all, were criminal cases that had become common place to her. Will had some great cases in the pipeline but was also a little bored with the day-today discovery slog. For both, the lack of trials for two people who feasted on them was discouraging.

Alex suggested he at least second chair one of the rape prosecutions and Will thought, if Rosalind and Jackie were OK with it, that might be an option at least to get him in the courtroom again.

They went to bed and cuddled and, for most of the night, slept as well as either of them could – Will deeply and Alex not so much. About 4:30, Alex woke to Will hysterically laughing still in his sleep. She shook him, he woke up and still was laughing hysterically. She could hear him in the bathroom, laughing his head off and, when he came back into the bedroom, she looked at him.

"So I had this dream, Alex." He started laughing again. "I was in a serious golf competition in which the elite players in the world – the world mind you – were in like a driving range and between the places where the golfers were going to hit, there were bleachers filled with the rich and famous. I mean, rich and famous. Everybody dressed in white. There were a series of clubs that each were to use starting with the driver and moving on to other clubs as the competition continued. Each stroke was for distance and accuracy. I was down toward the end of the line and, as each of the golfers ahead of me drove their balls deep into the fairway, there were 'oohs' and 'ahhs' from the crowd as the distance was measured off and accuracy down the fairway.

"It finally got to me, and I teed the ball up – which by the way you can do with a driver – shimmied my ass as I had seen others do it, stepped back, shimmied my ass some more, took aim and swung as hard as I could." He started to laugh again hard enough so that Alex began to join him. "Sadly, the only thing that flew was my club that flew at some incredible height and length diagonally towards some woods on the right side of the fairway. The ball, simply by the power of the swing, had toppled off the tee and lay beside it too close even to measure the distance. There was a deafening silence for a moment while everybody assimilated what had happened. Then I dropped to my knees and began to laugh. That started the fans, several whom fell out of their seats in hysterics, and soon everybody was gasping for breath.

"That's when I woke up."

By this time, Alex had joined Will in convulsions of laughter.

"You hate golf, Will."

"And I always will."

"Metaphor."

He nodded.

Too awake and still laughing too much, they checked the clock, let LacyB out for her morning duties, put their sweats on, and headed for the Frontier.

On the way over, Will said, in between giggles, "I have never in my life woken up from a deep sleep laughing my ass off, and still be laughing while I'm peeing, and then all the way back to bed."

"Write it down so you don't forget it, my love."

"Great idea."

Chapter Sixteen

Jorge

The next day Will had lunch with Jorge Herrera. Some years ago, Jorge had been on a path that ultimately would have led nowhere. Felipe Ruiz, who had spent several years in prison, took Jorge under his wing and had "scared the shit out of him" as Jorge would later put it. Felipe had married Jorge's mother, Rosie Herrera, and all was good until Felipe died. Jorge had been on the same crew with Felipe when he was killed in the cave-in in large part due to the greed of the company's owner.

Will had kept track of Jorge and his sister, Yolanda, and Rosie who had later married Ricky Storm, a corrections officer at North Prison, whose life Felipe had saved in the middle of a prison riot. Jorge had joined the Marines after graduating from high school and spent two tours in the Middle East. He was no longer a boy when he came back, got his bachelor's degree in three years from the University of New Mexico on the G.I. Bill, and started law school at UNM. He had graduated last December second in his class, having completed the course work in two and a half years, took the February bar exam, and was waiting for the results. He had already been promised a job at Johnston & Blackwell whether he passed the bar or not.

They met at Garcia's on Central at noon. Jorge looked every bit the Marine he had been, tall, lean and muscled, a brown handsome face with just a few lines at the corners of his eyes, and dark hair cut short like he'd had in the military. It was his brown eyes that caught Will's attention – they were his best feature, but Will would later tell Alex they were eyes that had seen a lifetime even though Jorge was not yet 30.

Jorge caught Will up on the family. Rosie and Ricky were doing great, Ricky had finally convinced his wife to quit her job at Garcia's after years of waitressing and she was working full time with the Foundation. Ricky was still in corrections but had almost enough time in to retire. Their plan, once Ricky retired, was to travel the United States in an Airstream. Yolanda had gotten a full ride scholarship to Stanford that the family always kidded her was because Stanford thought she was a foreign student from Mexico. Her plan was clinical counseling.

They got seated and Will asked, "When do you hear about the bar exam?"

"I passed, Will. Heard last Saturday."

"Great news, Jorge! The best!"

"Funny story, Will. My friends were calling Saturday morning saying they'd gotten the results and passed. Mine didn't come so I assumed they sent the failures out a day later. That afternoon I went to the post office for our neighborhood, and they were closed but I asked one of the cleaning people if she could help. Incredibly, she found it and then made me open the envelope in front of her to see if I passed or not. That's how I found out."

They both laughed. "Wonderful story." A pause. "Ready to go to work?"

"Tomorrow if possible."

Back when Will's partner, Luis Moreno, and Will had met Jorge and knew his dream was going to law school, both thought he'd be a great addition to Johnston & Blackwell. He'd made the rounds of the rest of the firm and there was no question they needed help. As well, there was no question about Jorge's work ethic and his brains. So, no brainer.

"Give us until Monday to get an office ready and get you set up. Enjoy the weekend. It'll be a while before you see another one."

Jorge laughed thinking it was a joke.

The next Monday, Jorge Herrera was introduced to the rest of the firm as the new associate. Rosalind, Jackie and Luis had all met him before, but he got introduced to everybody else and they had donuts and coffee in the breakroom. At noon, Rosalind and Jackie took him out to lunch. Part of it was taken up filling him in on the special prosecutor roles they had taken on and that they would need help on some of the cases. Jorge couldn't have been happier.

That afternoon, just about the time she was leaving, Will's long time legal assistant, Liz LaRue, knocked on his door.

"Hi, what's up, Liz?"

"Notice anything different about Rosalind today, Will?"

"Nope. What?"

Liz, for the millionth time, thought men were beyond redemption. "She had make up on and wore a skirt."

They had known each other for decades, from Michigan to New Mexico, and in all the years that he had known her, he had never once questioned her intuition about women.

"She's got something for Jorge."

He thought about it for a minute. He hadn't known Rosalind to date since her boyfriend had been killed helping young girls escape from being smuggled into the US from Mexico for sex slaves. But she and Jorge had known each other since the Felipe Ruiz trial, and he had been in the area for the last several years going to school after he had been discharged from the Marines. About the same age, give or take.

"Which one do we fire, Liz?"

"Neither, you idiot. Just saying. Good night, Will. Love to Alex."

"Night, Liz. Best to Duncan."

He thought about it for another minute. 'Hard to argue that one.'

Chapter Seventeen

The First Wave

Two weeks after the arrival of the 'traveling lab technicians' dubbed the 'Motown Five' by their co-workers, all of whom were put on the most recent cases, the lab had determined that there were fifty matches between victims and perpetrators who were already in the system. The easier of the tasks was to identify the whereabouts of the perps all of whom had current addresses in the probation office or, even easier, were in jail or prison on other charges. Seven of them had serial positive results meaning they had sexually assaulted more than one victim.

The more difficult was identifying where the victims were living. Of the fifty, the police and community agencies could only find addresses for forty-five. The other five were 'simply in the wind' presumably having moved to who knew where. Three others had died since the assaults – one suicide and two overdoses. Rawlings could only wonder if earlier intervention would have saved lives.

The District Attorney's office put together ten teams of volunteer social workers/clinical counselors matched with five of the sexual assault lawyers – up from three – and five of the volunteer special prosecutors , two of whom were Jackie and Rosalind.

All the social workers or clinical counselors were bilingual as was Rosalind. Thirteen of the initial twenty victims were Hispanic., four of whom did not speak

English. The interviews were excruciating, the women still in the anguish of what they had been through and, at the end of the day, fifteen agreed to cooperate and five declined. Not a great start but a good one.

A break came when the DNA results for Ricky Johnson, Ben Wise, and Mark Beland were added to the list. Johnson and Wise were identified as the two attackers in the sexual assaults taking place over the last several months on or around the UNM campus. All three were identified as being involved in the fraternity house gang rape some months ago.

Both Wise and Beland had been arraigned on the assault against Jackie LaPointe and, with the DNA matches, additional charges were added to Wise. Both were charged in the fraternity rape. All three came from wealthy families who were able to post bail and get their 'sweet' sons out of jail.

Chapter Eighteen

Two Down

Shortly before the end of the second semester at UNM, Ben Wise was walking with crutches across campus towards class. Both Achilles tendons had been operated on and he had been advised that the recovery would be long if – and it was a big if – the repairs held. By this time, he was able to put some weight bearing on his feet but was very unsteady even with his crutches.

He got to the classroom building without incident, attended class, and was going down the stairs to the first floor in a crush of students all hurrying to or from class. He had taken the first step down when he felt his left crutch slip out and a push in his back. He teetered and then fell forward knocking several students out of the way. He landed at the bottom of the stairs unconscious and bleeding from the back of his head.

Somebody called 911. By the time the police and ambulance arrived, Wise had still not regained consciousness and never would. The paramedics could not find a pulse and did everything they could but couldn't get him resuscitated. He died at the scene. An autopsy showed he died of a massive subdural hematoma caused by the fall. An incidental finding was that both repairs of his tendons had failed when he fell down the stairs.

Given the chaos in the stairwell, no one gave a thought that it might have been intentional and the only witness who might have said something was dead.

Chief of Homicide Margaret Espinoza was in her office at headquarters of the ABQ Police Department mulling over the rape kit investigation progress. It was not her division's case, and it wasn't like she didn't have a few other things to do but she had been involved from the start and was keeping track of events.

Espinoza had been a single mother and intending to stay single feeling that way even more so after her son died. Then she had met Rawlings and for the first time since her son's death had known joy. She had found her soul mate and had never known happiness could be so wonderful.

Her reverie was broken by a knock on the door and her chief assistant, Jorge Rodriguez, entered with a smile on his face.

"Caught another one, Chief."

She had known him too long to know what that smile meant.

"OK, Jorge, give it to me."

He read from his notes. "Older gentleman just turned himself in for murdering his wife. It was to have been a murder – suicide because his wife had cancer. He had hung her from one of the beams in their trailer at Sunnyside Trailer Park on Central close to Coors. Put her in bed afterwards and then tried the same thing on himself. Unfortunately, the beam wasn't high enough, so he tried the other one in the trailer, and it bent so his feet touched the floor. Next, he tried an old rifle but had two problems. No ammunition and he couldn't reach the trigger. Next, he tried sticking his head in the oven but had two problems. Stove was electric for one and the electricity had been turned off for non-payment for the other. Next, he filled the bathtub, got in, and threw the toaster oven in after him but had one problem. No electricity. Finally, he tried to cut his wrists but did it cross wise instead of length wise. Plus, he didn't hit the veins in either wrist. They bled a little bit and then clotted." He looked down at his notes clearly trying to stifle a laugh. "He spent three days sleeping in the same bed with his dead wife trying to figure out how to kill himself and then came here." He closed the notebook and looked at his chief.

Espinoza just shook her head. 'You can't make this shit up.'

"Wait 'til I tell my husband this one."

Chapter Nineteen

We Did, We Do

On the one-week anniversary of Jorge Herrera's joining the firm, he and Rosalind appeared at Will's office door.

"I'm pregnant."

"I'm the father."

In unison, "Do you think Judge Kennedy would marry us?"

Will felt time slow down in which seconds seemed like hours. A lot to take in about 5 seconds – his rock star was pregnant, his brand new can't miss rock star was the father - and they wanted his wife to marry them. The last piece was the easiest – it was the first two bits of news that would take a little longer. He knew he should say something wise and warm and wonderful. The best he could do?

"Wow." Another pause that seemed to last forever.

"So how did all this happen?" Realizing as soon as he said it, how stupid that was. Of course, he knew how it had happened. Jesus.

Rosalind saved him. "As you know, we met when we were working on Felipe's case. When Jorge went in the Marines and when he was overseas, we would write each other sporadically and then when he came back, we dated a little bit while he was in undergrad. And then steadily through law school.

"Why didn't you tell me?"

"Great question, Will. Fear mostly but then I got pregnant, and we hired Jorge and we decided the time had come. Jackie knew. Nobody else."

"Well, first and foremost, congratulations." Will was finding his footing. "Of course, Alex will marry you and be thrilled you'd ask. When are you due?"

"Late November or early December, Will."

He nodded, thinking to himself that if they both took maternity/paternity leave, his practice was pretty well screwed.

"When would you like to get married?"

"As soon as possible," again in unison. "Today?"

"Three day waiting period?"

"We got the license last Wednesday."

"Let me check with the Judge."

"Thanks, Will, so much." They were both crying and Will felt tears welling up as well.

And so it came to be that that Monday afternoon at 4:00 PM in Judge Kennedy's chambers, Rosalind and Jorge were married.

Karen Stillson, Alex's Case Manager, ushered the bride and groom in right at 4:00. Waiting were the judge, Jackie LaPointe, Will, Rosie and Ricky Storm, and Yolanda from Stanford via Zoom.

Preliminaries done, the vows and rings exchanged, Judge Kennedy ended the celebration with these words.

"You two at way too young an age have been faced with the worst tragedies life can deal you. But you both have persevered and in perseverance have forged the strength and courage in each other that will bind you forever. Your child will inherit that strength and courage. Godspeed. You may kiss each other."

Alex had smuggled in a bottle of champagne from the parking garage, and it was poured into Styrofoam coffee cups for a quick toast to the newlyweds. Yolanda joined them with a glass of wine from Palo Alto.

Dinner after at a private room at Scalo on Central. Ubers home.   Except for Rosalind and Jorge.

Chapter Twenty

Lieutenant Sheila Jackson

One of the very few female African American officers in the Albuquerque Police Department, Detective Jackson, like Margaret Espinoza, had worked her way up through the ranks. Married to a lawyer with one of the big firms in Albuquerque who was scared to death for his wife every time she went to work. Two kids who thought it was really 'cool' their mom was a cop.

Even the most racist officers in the ABQ had to admit she had guts. Three years after she joined the force, Jackson and her partner were on patrol in the War Zone, southeast of downtown, when they were ambushed by a group from one of the infamous Alvarez local gangs whose initiation for young members was to kill a cop.

In the initial barrage, Jackson's partner, who was driving, was wounded by the automatic weapons the gang were using when the windows on the driver's side of the patrol car were blown out. She got him out the passenger door, called it in, and then took cover behind the patrol car, returned fire, and calmly killed five of the gang members. Whoever was left quickly fled the scene just as help was arriving.

Sgt. Rodriguez was the first Sergeant on the scene and took control calling for a 'bus' to get the wounded officer to the hospital. He was conscious and lucid and there was little blood, all good signs. Other officers began to canvas the neighborhood but, as usual, nobody saw or heard anything.

Crime scene officers arrived and started their investigation. The medical examiner began work on the bangers' bodies. Unfortunately, none of them was Eduardo Alvarez, head of the gang.

One of the crime scene technicians walked up to Rodriguez and asked to have a moment.

"We only found eight shell cases where Jackson was."

The Sergeant raised an eyebrow.

"Eight shell cases and she killed five of them with five of the eight shots."

"Efficient. Helping save money for the department.'

He walked over to where Jackson was being evaluated by the EMTs.

"You OK?"

"Fine, Sergeant. George?" Her partner.

"Initial report from the ER, he's doing fine. Nothing major hit. You saved his life.'

She shrugged. He paused and would never admit it but teared up just for a second. God, he loved being a cop.

"Damn good shooting, Officer.'

She smiled. "Not really. None of them had bothered to take cover."

He smiled back. "Right."

Three years later, she was promoted to Lieutenant. Sgt. Rodriguez tried to talk her into Homicide, but she wanted the Sex Crimes Unit. Her younger sister, age 11, had been kidnapped, raped and murdered several years before. For Sheila Jackson, this was about her sister…and revenge.

All of which led her to be lead on the assault on Jackie LaPointe. She first visited Mark Beland in the hospital after he had been stitched up. It was a short visit. His mother and father were in the room, mother was a lawyer in Santa Fe, and advised Lieutenant Jackson her son would not talk until she had hired a lawyer for him. It didn't bother her much – not her first science project as she liked to say – because they had his DNA at the attack in the alley plus the gang rape at the fraternity house. Be a long time before he got his college degree.

She also visited Ben Wise who was waiting for surgery on his tendons. His father from Farmington was with him and had the same advice for his son – lawyer up. Didn't matter for him either.

She never did get to see Ricky Johnson. He had already died from his wounds on the operating table. Sheila Jackson smiled to herself. First lesson learned was don't mess with Jackie LaPointe. Second lesson learned was for Jackson to be fitted for an ankle knife sheath; it would go on her left ankle because the right ankle carried the backup gun. She reminded herself to lose a couple of pounds to make up for the extra weight of the knife.

Two weeks later, she was in the Steven Schiff Office Building in a conference room in the District

Attorney's office with J.D. Rawlings, Alice Robbins, Mark Beland, his parents, and Richard (don't call me Dick) Shorter, Beland's defense lawyer.

Beland was only able to use his left arm, the right one held stiffly to his body to hopefully hold the staples in his side in place to give his abdomen a chance to heal. To Jackson, even only two weeks later, Beland looked terrible – much thinner, gray complexion, sunken eyes, clearly almost near tears.

Rawlings. "I understand you think he's a good 'kid,' Richard, but we have him dead to rights on both the alley attack and the gang rape. No priors, fair student, big time jock in high school. OK. But somehow in the last couple of years he has turned bad – Fraternity? Bad friends? Too much beer? Fact remains, he's become a menace and is going to prison. We're willing to recommend eighteen years at North for both crimes with time off for good behavior."

Beland and his father both started to cry. His mother showed no emotion whatsoever.

"Jesus Christ, J.D., that'd be like throwing raw meat to the wolves." Shorter immediately wished he'd picked a better metaphor.   The Beland men went from crying to sobbing.

"If he gives us the names of the other frat boys who gang raped the drunk freshman co-ed, we might be able to recommend something less than twenty, but we'll still recommend prison time. We know it was Beland and his two buddies, but we think there were at least five others, maybe more. 'Course it's up to the judge."

Shorter and his client and parents excused themselves and left the conference room. They were back in five minutes.

"He'll give you the names."

They finally decided on a recommendation of nine years for both crimes with time off but with no guarantees from the judge. What Shorter didn't know was that this judge had a daughter who was a sophomore at UNM in the same sorority as the victim.

Just before the end of classes, Beland was walking across campus with his right arm still straight and close to his side. From behind him, he felt somebody grab the arm and pull it straight up. He screamed from the pain in his side, felt it turn immediately wet, and collapsed to the ground.

He caught a glimpse of the person. They were wearing a Clown mask and they turned and disappeared into the student crowd as people rushed to help Beland.

Two months later after rehab, he and his parents were told that, with three blood transfusions, the doctors were able to stitch Beland's side back together but with the formation of the scar tissue in his abdominal muscles, he would never be able to move his right arm more than three to six inches from his side.

A month after that, an unsympathetic judge sentenced Beland to 15 years each on the two crimes, the sentences to run concurrently.

Shorter had been right about prison. It was like throwing raw meat to the wolves. Three days after he got there, he was gang raped in the prison shower, the first of many. Two days after about the tenth attack, he hung himself in his cell.

Irony.

Shortly after the meeting in J.D.'s office, the police got warrants for DNA samples from the five frat boys Beland had named. They were a match and all five were charged with second degree sexual assault, pled guilty, and received five years each. The fifth went to trial with the defense that the DNA wasn't his and there had been a mistake in the lab. Pretty good defense given the history of the lab's problems. The jury in twenty minutes said he was wrong, and he was sentenced to the maximum of nine years. Raw meat as well.

And for the victim of the assault? With the support of friends and family and counselors, she recovered physically and psychologically as much as possible, never took another drink in her life, and devoted herself to counseling young women on what might lie ahead as a part of the orientation for incoming freshman at the University of New Mexico. At her insistence, the course was mandatory. And when she wasn't teaching, she was counseling when the lesson she had learned didn't take.

Chapter Twenty-One

Breakthrough?

J.D. months later would return to the attack on Jackie LaPointe as a turning point in the rape kit scandal. Days after the attack and after the three young men had been charged in the attack, J.D, the Mayor, and Chief Johnson called a second press conference announcing the arrest of the three men based on their DNA and the fact that the three men had been wounded, one of them having died in the aftermath. Jackie's name was never mentioned but, in her anonymity, she became a hero to women in general and sexual assault victims especially.

Still working overtime and deciding that working on the oldest cases was not time well spent, Lab Director Connery concentrated all the technicians, including the 'Motown Five,', on the most recent cases working backwards. There were always new cases to be added to the lists as sexual assaults continued in New Mexico but while DNA matches continued, law enforcement began to see a subtle shift in how many women were willing to come forward. Plus, there were two changes in the way the cases were investigated. The 20% 'don't believe the victim' was a thing of the past. The 20% of 'can't find the victim' would only be accepted after a thorough search was undertaken and signed off by the officers' C.O.s if they were unsuccessful. The percentages dropped precipitously.

Rawlings was never sure whether it was the press conference on progress or Jackie's example, but something was changing and to the good.

Neither his office nor the APQ Police Department Sex Crimes Unit were tracking what, in the days to come, would become a very strange trend. The decision was made to only arrest those men whose DNA matched the DNA found on the victims who were willing to come forward or, in the cases of serial rapists, only if at least one of the victims came forward. It made perfect sense. They would worry about the other perps when there were more resources.

What they didn't know was that the group whose DNA had been identified without victim co-operation were either disappearing or being killed in what were seemingly random crimes mostly connected to gang and drug violence. Four men were never found and three more were killed by gun shots. The disappearances were, after talking with relatives or friends, chalked up to leaving the state having read the headlines about the investigation underway. The killings were also investigated but no suspects were found, ballistics couldn't confirm anything, and they quickly became cold cases. The victims were kept up to date.

The first possible break came some weeks later when a witness came forward and said that he'd seen one of the men who disappeared – number eight now – drive off in a grey SUV in the passenger seat. He couldn't give any description of the driver and didn't think to look at the license plate. His friend was never seen again.

Three more DNA matches were also killed, two by guns and one by knife.

Seven men killed and eight disappeared and the only thing they had in common was that their DNA had been connected to a sexual assault in the last six years in the greater Albuquerque area.

That caught the attention of Margaret Espinoza. She was a woman who didn't believe in coincidences especially when it came to homicides and this was a spike in homicides out of the norm for any given year. She asked for a meeting with the District Attorney.

In attendance the next day were the District Attorney, the Assistant District Attorney in charge of the DNA investigation, the Chief of Homicide, the Assistant Chief of Homicide, and the lead lieutenant of the Sex Crimes Unit.

Espinoza had called for the meeting and started it.

"We now have 15 men who have disappeared or been killed, and the only connection is a match between their DNA and the DNA of victims who won't co-operate. Random geographics except that most of the killings – five of them – have been in the southwest part of town. She referred to the map they had taped to the wall with red pins. Missing are from all over the place noted with blue pins.

"Vigilantes? Has to be more than one given the number of victims," said Robbins.

They all nodded.

Rodriguez. "And an inside job. It would have to be to know which perps should be targeted."

Silence. "The trouble is there are a lot of people on the inside," said Rawlings. "The D.A.'s office, the Sex Crimes Unit, the Crime Lab. There are dozens who could have, did have, or will have access to the information all of whom could be the group of vigilantes."

Detective Jackson spoke. "To play the Devil's Advocate and realizing this will put me at the top of the list of suspects, who cares what happens to these assholes? We all know they're guilty based on the DNA, we know they've escaped for years for some of them because of the backlog, and now we know that at least the ones that have been killed have been brought to justice. Who cares?"

There was a longer silence this time because all of them in the room agreed with her. They had it coming regardless of whether their victims would come forward or not. But.

"We all agree, Lieutenant, 100%. But all of us in the room are the rule of law. And we can't let vigilantes substitute themselves for us. That's the simple answer. Did I mention I agree with you?

"From here on out, we restrict access to the results and cut down the number of people who have access. It's ain't perfect but it's best we can do. We work our asses off to try to get a handle on 5,000 untested rape kits, thanks to all of you we make progress, and then we get double crossed by a group that takes the law into their own hands," said Rawlings.

That night, in the cool of the July New Mexico evening, J.D. and Margaret sat on their balcony with a dry martini for each and tried to piece it together, two veterans who had arrested and prosecuted thousands of defendants. Not their first rodeo.

"Men or women or both," Margaret started.

"Women."

"Why?"

"Revenge."

"So the group has a history of sexual abuse?"

"Yep, but where does it get us? Every woman in our groups either has been assaulted herself or knows somebody who has been. And when you think about it, so do most men know somebody. Still think it's women."

"With enough force to disappear men or kill them? Especially violent men?"

"Fair. If there were more than one?"

"Maybe. A gun would help." Margaret thought for a moment. "If you ever repeat this beyond this balcony, I'll kill you, but these men are not only violent but sexual predators. What if we put in the mix that it's a woman or women and they are using their sex to lure these men into compromising situations where they can be kidnapped or killed? One of the guys we can't find was last seen being driven away. What if it were a promise for sex?"

"Glad you said it, my love. Women who are good looking, using their sex to lure the perps, and then killing or disappearing them. You got a sense of race?"

"Nope. The perps are all colors as are the victims. Only thing we've got going for us is that the demographics in Albuquerque favor either white or brown. I suppose we could look at the groups that would have had access to the information." She paused. "Geez, all my life I've battled racial profiling among our police department and here I am. Cut me off."

"Can we at least eliminate the lab people?"

"Nope, I talked to Mary Elizabeth today. When the techies are done, the results go in two piles, one of which is where the victims will come forward and one where they won't. Never dawned on any of us when we started this journey that we'd be looking at a serial killer."

"So to sum up, we're looking for attractive women who have been sexually assaulted or know somebody close to them who has been who use feminine wiles and a gun to lure sociopaths so they can kidnap them or kill them. Would a second martini help?"

"Nope. Plus we'd probably forget what we just talked about."

"Mac and cheese?"

"Perfect."

Meanwhile, not very far away in Old Town, the exact same discussion was being had on the patio at Alex and Will's townhouse. Except over Jameson's on the rocks instead of Tito's martinis up.

Alex had roughly added up all the people in the D.A.'s office, the ABQ Police, and the Crime Lab and had come to the rough conclusion that there were several hundred people who could have had access to the reports if one added in all the people like support staff, paralegals, clerks, etc. If the conclusion was that it was a woman or women, that would cut the number in just about half. Weeks ago when the news hit about the backlog in 5,000 rape kits that had never been tested, no one had given a thought that a serial killer would go after only those perps who had been identified but without co-operation from victims for whatever reason. There were just too many other things to worry about and concentrate on. Safeguards were now in place to limit access as the tests went on but there were still many perps that potentially were in harm's way.

"Tell me it's not Jackie, Will."

"I know, I wish I could, but I can't."

There was much about Jackie LaPointe's past that was simply off limits. Alex and Will knew she had been raised in several foster care homes, had run away the first time she could, and had lived on the streets for several years before she landed a job as an intern with the Alexandria, Virginia Police Department. They both knew there was an anger in Jackie that was just below the surface and usually only made itself known when she sensed injustice. Like when she was attacked in the alley. Or like when somebody she loved was threatened.

"I mean, come on, Will. How many lawyers do you know who have knives in an ankle sheath?"

He nodded. "Another drink?"

"Nope, too much work to do after dinner."

"Mac and cheese?"

"Perfect."

Chapter Twenty Two

Frustration

Meanwhile, over on Knob Hill at a bar on Central cleverly called the Bar just east of the UNM campus, Jackie, Rosalind ('don't call me Herrera, my name is McManus and always will be'), and Jorge were having drinks, beers for Jackie and Jorge and tonic for Rosalind.

Like all the members of the Sexual Assault Strike Team, Jackie and Rosalind were chomping at the bit to get 'one of these mother fuckers to trial' as Jackie so delicately put it.

What they hadn't anticipated was that once the dam began to break and perps were identified, the process became one more criminal case in the process. The energy that started the project slowly dissipated as defendants got lawyers, arraignments and discovery issues were handled by the D.A.'s office, a lack of co-operation by some victims, and the unexpected depletion of potential defendants by disappearance and killings. Another factor that the special prosecutors hadn't factored in was the number of plea deals that the defendants were trying to reach with the prosecution. Once the DNA was matched and the victim agreed to co-operate, there was little upside in going to trial.

Rosalind and Jackie were to handle a case that was scheduled for trial in late October against Eduardo Alvarez, the head of the Alvarez gang which had been decimated in the shootout with now Lieutenant Jackson and which bumped into Rosalind's due date. Jorge had volunteered to co-counsel, a gesture that went down in spectacular flames when his wife got wind of it. At the request of the defense, the case had been adjourned to give it more time to prepare and to respond to discovery from the prosecutor. Jackie assigned to be lead counsel was excited and exhilarated. Will volunteered to second chair, a request taken under advisement by lead counsel – Jackie LaPointe.

Back at the ranch, there was plenty of work to do. A week after they were married, Jorge Herrera was sworn into the bar in a special ceremony presided over by the Chief Judge, Alexandra Kennedy. In attendance was the entire firm, Jorge's parents, Jackie's spouse and daughter, and many of his classmates from law school who, over time, had learned of Jorge's history and his tours in the Middle East. When Judge Kennedy finally was done with the oath and said, "Welcome to the Bar, Mr. Herrera," the audience gave him a standing ovation. Including the Judge.

After that, Will's comment weeks ago about weekends became fact. The good news was that it gave Rosalind and Jorge time together and helped Jackie look forward to the times in the office. It didn't hurt that Will Bennett, among others, was usually there on Saturday and the firm often bought lunch for those who were around. As long as they didn't just come for the lunch.

In plaintiffs' personal injury cases, success breeds success and the team at Johnston & Blackwell had had some very stunning successes not the least of which was the Ruiz trial which, midst the tragedy of Felipe Ruiz's cave in death, had resulted in the 18-million-dollar verdict against the company that employed him. That had resulted in several new cases coming in the door and Will and his group were careful to screen the cases to take the ones that had a reasonable chance of success at settlement or trial or ones that the firm felt were worth taking a flyer at to find justice if not money. Will, from Michigan where advertising was ethical but seldom done, had no use for the billboards or sides of buses that advertised for lawyers in New Mexico. So far, they hadn't needed to.

The 'bread and butter' for plaintiffs' attorneys was I-25 North and South to and from Santa Fe and Albuquerque/ The number of bad accidents and resulting injuries and deaths explained, in large part, the number of corresponding billboards for personal injury lawyers in the same stretch.

Chapter Twenty Three

Progress

The next day, J.D. and Alice Robbins met to go over the progress for the first seven months. Of the original 5,000 untested kits, 1,000 of the cases were too old and too cold and had been closed. Of the most recent 1,400 cases, 900 of them had been tested and had resulted in identifying 600 potential defendants who were still alive. Of the other 300 remaining, 125 had died either of violence or 'other' which usually meant violence but couldn't be proved, 150 were in prison on other felony charges that ranged from armed robbery to murder, and 25 couldn't be found. Of those in prison, if the offender would remain in prison longer than any possible sentence on the new sexual assault charges, and if the victims were OK with it, those cases were dropped. In seven months, the task force had cut the backlog almost in half.

They were on a roll.

There was a knock on the door and Julie Stahl walked into the conference room. She handed a note to J.D. who read it and gave it to Robbins.

The Sheriff of Sandoval County had called her counterpart in Bernalillo County to report that a homeowner just north of Placitas in the Sandia foothills had called in and said their German Shepard had proudly brought a long bone to the back door that morning. It wasn't unusual for the dog to find bones among other things but this one was a little different. It had pieces of fragment on it that looked a lot like part of a pair of pants.

She had driven it to the Sheriff's Department in Bernalillo County who had taken it to the Medical Examiner's office. Initial finding was that it was a human tibia, a long bone in the lower human leg. The fabric was denim. DNA findings were pending.

J.D and Alice Robbins looked at each other. "Well," he said, "it's a start."

Later that day, the Medical Examiner called J.D. and reported that the DNA from the tibia matched one of the perps who had disappeared.

Over the next several days, K9 units from the Sheriffs' Departments of Sandoval and Bernalillo Counties scoured the area north and south of Placitas. The units found human remains of three or four others whose DNA matched up with the lab results. All in all, progress but disappointing. None of the remains were attached to any other remains and none identified any DNA other than the remains.

After telling Margaret, J.D. made the decision not to release the discovery to the public. The day after the public knew, the area would be inundated with hundreds of people trampling through the area and neighborhoods with everything from shovels to metal detectors to Tarot cards to incense. Land of Enchantment.

Chapter Twenty Three

Margaret

Margaret was at her desk reviewing the mayhem in Albuquerque over the weekend trying to decide the priorities of investigating the several shootings, only one of which fortunately had resulted in a potential homicide. Two others were accidental discharges by the person holding the gun, one was a seven-year-old who shot his mother in the arm by accident, and one was road rage where two men (of course) got angry at each other on Lomas driving side by side, pulled over into a parking lot, got out, took out guns and began to shoot at each other. They emptied their magazines without hitting anything other than a couple of buildings and the cars they were standing next to until the last bullet in both guns hit the other guy in the foot. It was not life threatening. During the entire confrontation, they were six feet away from each other.

She finally had one she could share with Jorge rather than the other way around.

On a whim, she got to thinking about the rape kit project and the disappearing perps and the one witness who had seen one of those who had disappeared get into a car and drive away with somebody. She asked Jorge to search the area for security cameras that might still have footage of the area on that date. Just a hunch.

The nice thing about being in a high crime area was that almost all commercial and residential buildings had security cameras. She asked Jorge to assign some officers to canvas the neighborhood and see if they could find security video on the night the man disappeared in the gray SUV. A day later, the police had found four different videos which promptly went from Homicide to the Technical Assistance Recovery Unit (TARU) or, as Margaret liked to call it, 'The Geek Unit.' She was particularly interested in the driver, the make of the car, and the license plate.

That afternoon, she met with the chief 'Geek' who told her what they had found. The SUV was a late model Honda, the New Mexico license plate was indecipherable even under the highest magnification except for a 'T' at the beginning, and the driver, while wearing a baseball cap and sunglasses had blond hair below the neckline. Impossible to tell if it was a man or a woman.

Back to her office, she checked her 'To Be Saved' file and found the report on Jerry Kent, the suicide from months before who used the wrong hand to kill himself. Was he the first?

That night, she and J.D. noodled what the TARU found and came up with a working profile. They were looking for a man or woman with blond hair acting alone who was from New Mexico and who was well enough off to drive a late model car. Margaret also had access to the files that distinguished between those in which the victims were co-operating and those who weren't. And, unless the blond hair was a wig or a bleach job, she was most likely Caucasian.

They had earned themselves a Tito's.

Mid-morning the next day, J.D. walked through the secure parking garage in the basement of the Schiff Office Building where the District Attorney lawyers parked. There were a couple of SUVs that were gray but only one that was a late model Honda that had a New Mexico license plate that began with a 'T.'

Back in his office, he ran the plate. The car belonged to Alice Robbins.

He called his wife and told her, then sat in his office in utter disbelief. He had known Robbins for years and they had been colleagues as Assistant District Attorneys. A very good trial lawyer and someone he considered a friend and now somebody that matched the working hypothesis he and Margaret had put together right down to the shoulder-length blonde hair.

Margaret and J.D. met for lunch at the Church Street Café in Old Town behind the church. Reputed to be one of the oldest buildings in Albuquerque, the café catered to the tourist business during tourist season but come summertime when the heat ('but it's a dry heat') came to the valley, the locals took it over. They sat indoors with the beautiful rugs on the walls, Southwestern art, and the roughhewn wooden tables and chairs and looked out on the brick patio, now deserted in the high noon heat.

Neither would remember later what they ordered although they knew it would be good. They weren't there for the food but to decide what to do next.

Rawlings started. "If, if, if we're right and Robbins is one of the vigilantes, two questions. One, do we care what they've done, eliminating vermin we know are guilty of rape? And if the answer to that question is yes, how do we ever prove it? Hell, how would we ever go to a judge and ask for warrant?"

Margaret studied the bowl of chips and salsa in front of them for a long time as though it were the best bowl of chips and salsa she had ever seen. She finally looked up and looked at her husband. .

"The cop in me says we run it to ground if we can. It's what we do and are sworn to do." She was reminded of the cold case of four brutal, evil men who were murdered and whose file now was more than 'cold.' Wasn't this the same thing? Vigilante justice for a just cause. Why not? "But even if we're right and we try to run it to ground, how to do it is the far bigger question unless they mess up. And she certainly has not made any mistakes except for the eyewitness and the security tapes. Not even close to charging her."

He nodded as the food arrived. Green chili cheeseburger and fries for him and green chili stew for her. Soul food.

"I guess the good news is that there is an end to this. I have no idea how many more victims will decline to co-operate and so how many perps will go free, but sooner or later, it's over."

"Well, sure, J.D. but does that mean another dozen men killed? Two dozen? More? A question back to you, my love. What if we knew this was the end? Would we still try to run the vigilantes to ground? Even if we could?"

They ate in silence, each with their own thoughts and each comfortable enough with each other to let it be.

After the dishes were cleared, they both started to talk at the same time, and laughed.

"You go first, J.D. This would never happen in my division."

They laughed again, both thinking 'right, Margaret, whatever you say.'

He nodded. "As we sit here today, it's only the two of us who have come to this. What if I have a meeting with Alice Robbins, tell her we're making some real progress thanks to your office on identifying the vigilantes, include a statement from the eyewitness, add in the security tapes, leave out a few parts...like the license plate and the blond hair. See what happens."

"You're a mind reader, you jerk! You stole my idea!" She threw her napkin down on the table in a mock rage. "Goddamn it, Rawlings." An older couple at the next table looked over. 'Ohio tourists,' he thought to himself.

"Sorry, folks, my wife gets a little unhinged at times." He turned back to Margaret who looked like she was about to launch the chip basket at him. "So we come full circle. Let's say our plan works and the killings stop. Then what? Do we care? How do we prove it?"

He asked for the check.

"I'd like a few more heads thinking about this but don't know who we could ask. Alex? Judge? and it wouldn't be fair to ask her.   Will? Friend but his associates are prosecutors in the SAKI project. Jorge? Maybe. At least he's not blond. Anybody else and we worry about leaks and then we're nowhere."

The check came and J.D. reached for his wallet. "Oh geez, Margaret, I left my wallet at the office. Could you do this?" He handed her the check. She took it and turned to the people from Ohio. "Biggest grifter this side of the Mississippi. I don't think he even owns a wallet."

She turned back and paid.

On the way to their cars, Margaret had a thought. "Of all of the special prosecutors who are dying on the vine, who are the ones most invested and most helpful in the process?"

"Easy. Jackie LaPointe and Rosalind McManus. Why?"

Well, we can't run this by anybody in my division or your office. You trust them enough to sit down with them, swear them to secrecy, and tell them what you think? Both lawyers, both well respected, and both invested."

"Good thought. Lemme think about it. Thanks for lunch – again. See you at home. Love you."

"Love you."

That evening he texted both Rosalind and Jackie and asked them to meet him for breakfast at the Western View out on Central almost to Coors at 7:30. They both accepted, as did Noni, because Josephine was working a 24-hour shift at the hospital.

On the dot the next morning, the four of them convened. Breakfasts ordered, a sippy cup on board, J.D. first swore them to secrecy as special prosecutors, and then laid out everything he knew up to and including the TARU enhancements of the car and driver.

"Alice Robbins as part of a vigilante group. Wow." Rosalind. Noni nodded in agreement.

It took Jackie a minute to think out what she was going to say. "There's something you don't know, J.D., and I think you need to know it because it's an important piece of the puzzle. Alice Robbins told us she was gang raped by members of the Colorado State football team when she was a freshman. She made it her career goal to go to law school and become a prosecutor working on sex crimes. To our knowledge, she has never married, no kids, lives alone and her job is her life. It fits."

"If you were me, what would you do?

Rosalind. "Part of me wants to put up a statue in her honor and part of me thinks she's no better than the people she's killed. If it's true. Trouble is and I haven't been a lawyer for a long time, but I'm guessing that whoever got this case to prosecute – because it won't be you – doesn't have a chance for a guilty verdict or even enough to charge."

Jackie and Noni both agreed. That was the issue.

Chapter Twenty Five

Alice

Later that morning, J.D. knocked on Robbins' door and was invited in.

"Hi Chief, what's up?"

"We're making progress, Alice, and I wanted to bring you up to date." He did, leaving out only a couple of small details – like the 'T' on the license plate and the color of the hair of the driver – but everything else he filled in. "We're getting there. TARU is still working on further enhancements in the hopes we can get the license plate."

Alice Robbins nodded and said, "That's great, Chief. Great." Flat.

He stood up to leave. "I'll keep you posted, Alice." Left and closed her door behind him.

If he were honest, Rawlings would agree to a certain smugness on how that went as he walked back to his office. If Alice was one of them.

The trap was set.

That afternoon, Rawlings walked by Robbins' office and the Do Not Disturb sign was on. Two days later, he walked through the parking garage and saw what looked to be a brand-new KIA. No sign of the gray Honda. He ran the plate, and it was an Enterprise Rental car. Two days after that, there was a brand-new Subaru Legacy in the garage. That plate was registered to Alice Robbins.

Two weeks went by, and additional positive connections in the lab were made between DNA results found and perpetrators. In several of the cases, the victims would not co-operate. None of those men were either murdered or disappeared.

Until a month later. The crime lab reported that a match had occurred between the DNA recovered as a result of a rape kit test several months before and one of the potential perpetrators, George Duncan. There would be no charges brought because the victim had died. The name of the victim was Leslie Helm. That name meant nothing to anyone involved in the investigation except for one person.

A week later, George Duncan's naked body was found in a dumpster. Death was by his throat being sliced down to the spinal cord but what was even more chilling was that the M.E. reported that he had been castrated with the same knife while he was still alive. Testicles and penis were never recovered. The murder weapon was never found, and no one was ever charged.

Both Espinoza and Rawlings had looked at the report when it came in and concluded it was not Alice Robbins because the viciousness of the attack didn't come close to matching any of the deaths of the other perps they thought she had caused. Plus, they still had her under surveillance.

Lieutenant Sheila Davidson had seen that kind of viciousness once before in her career but saw no reason to mention it to anybody.

Chapter Twenty Six

Diedre McManus Herrera

On October 24, a new baby was ushered into the world. Diedre McManus Herrera was born at 11:00 PM weighing in at 8lbs, 6 ounces. Mom and daughter were doing fine and father was resting comfortably after having passed out rather spectacularly in the delivery suite. No surprise to anyone, Rosalind had declined any anesthetic – which may in part have caused the sudden departure from consciousness of her husband, Jorge.

Diedra was named after Rosalind's mother who had died at age 34 of ovarian cancer. Unbeknownst to many, including Will and the other members of the law firm, Rosalind had been raised by her aunt and uncle into adulthood, but they had been killed in a car accident when a drunk driver had hit them head on. Rosalind was on her own. She was 21. No wonder she was tough.

The day after Diedre was born, there was a steady stream of visitors, including Jackie, Josephine and Noni as well as Will and Alex, members of the firm, friends and neighbors and, of course, the new grandparents, Rosie and Ricky. Yolanda arrived for a long weekend and welcomed her niece into the family. Joyous times. Only Jackie seemed a bit distracted although it had been her who had planned the baby shower at the firm two weeks before. 'A very good haul' as Jackie would later describe it.

Chapter Twenty Seven

October

One of the many things Jackie LaPointe had learned at the knee of Will Bennett was how to get ready for trial and, as the case against Eduardo Alvarez, head of the Alvarez gang, got closer to trial, those lessons were well learned. She knew that the key was to prepare for everything you could and then get ready for the unknown that you hadn't prepared for when it came up at trial. That's what she did. Initially, Alice Robbins was to have second chaired the case with Jackie, but she ended up with an irreconcilable conflict and, with Rosalind out on maternity leave, Jackie was on her own.

Will stepped up and if Jackie didn't want him in the courtroom, he did everything he could to help her get ready. He underscored the lessons she had already learned, spent hours talking about themes and theories, about the questions Jackie should put to the jury on jury selection, the instructions that were to be given to the jury at the end of the trial, the demeanor of the judge (a woman) and whether she was going to be strong enough to keep order in what was likely to be, at best, contentious, and a dozen other issues in the run up to trial.

Eduardo Alvarez's DNA had matched the DNA taken from three victims as a part of the rape kit examinations and, in addition, it had been found in two of the three apartments in Albuquerque where the attacks had taken place. Two of the three victims had agreed to testify, the third having declined to do so. Ramon was well known in the War Zone as the leader of the gang that had ambushed Officer Jackson and her partner, five of whom had died that night when Jackson returned fire. Even with that setback, Alvarez thought he was Teflon Man that no women in their right minds who lived in the War Zone would ever testify against him.

A week in trial proved just how wrong he could be.

Alvarez was represented by an experienced criminal defense attorney, Donald Jenkins, who himself had been a District Judge, before resigning in disgrace just before he had been charged with solicitation of prostitutes on East Central on the edge of the War Zone. Jenkins had done very well for himself representing pimps and prostitutes and was commanding a hefty retainer these days unless there was something to barter with, usually involving the prostitutes. He took on the Alvarez case for a $25,000 retainer that was paid in cash. He didn't want to know where the money came from.

Jenkins had made it very clear to Mr. Alvarez that the results of the DNA from the rape kits at the hospital as well as the DNA found at the scenes were very problematic, but Alvarez insisted on trial. He also insisted on testifying in his own defense, a decision that Jenkins vehemently opposed.

Jury selection took a full day. Jackie had decided that the main thing was to get women on the jury and, if men, make certain they had daughters. Of the fourteen seated, with twelve to decide the case and two alternates, there were 8 women and six men all of whom had daughters.   She was pleased.

The trial itself took three days and consisted of the nurses at the hospitals where the rape kits were done, the DNA experts to testify to the match with Alvarez, and the two victims. They sat with Jackie the whole trial at counsel table and the jury was riveted to them even before they testified. She got them on and off as quickly as she could, but both were surprisingly strong and kept their eyes on Alvarez at defense counsel's table for most of their testimony. He wouldn't return their glares. Jenkins was no dummy and chose not to cross examine any of the prosecution witnesses. There was no point.

At the close of the prosecution's case, Alvarez took the witness stand in his own defense. He testified that the sex with the victims had been consensual and, in both cases, had been because the victims approached him at the bar where his gang hung out. Gilding the lily and with Jenkins cringing every step of the way, the defendant talked at length about his sexual prowess and about how often women would solicit him for sex. He talked about the good things he had done in the community where he lived, none of which he could remember specifically, and that, at heart, he was a pillar of the War Zone community.

Will Bennett came to the trial to specifically watch Jackie cross examine Alvarez. He had worried about Jackie's emotional state during the trial and whether her anger would get the best of her. He shouldn't have worried. She was professional, calm, and handled especially the direct examinations of the victims with both empathy and professionalism. Her cross examination of Alvarez was textbook with a witness who wouldn't know the truth if it bit him. She got him to admit that it was not a rare event for him to have sex with three or four different women in a day, a statement the jury collectively rolled their eyes at and, in one instance, drew a laugh from one of the male jurors. He also admitted to being the leader of a gang who did wonderful things for the community and testified that it was police brutality that had killed five of the members of the gang.

On rebuttal, Jackie called the police officer who was injured in the attack, Sheila Jackson, and an expert witness who testified each of the gang members were armed with AK 15 automatic rifles. Her coup de grace was calling a formal gang member who testified that, in order to become a member of the gang and, over objection by Alvarez's counsel, Alvarez ordered they had to kill a police officer. 'Wonderful things' for the community' indeed.

Jackie LaPointe's closing argument was done in the same professional and calm manner as the rest of her presence. On rebuttal, her sit down moment was this:

"Ladies and Gentlemen. This case isn't about a 'reasonable doubt' because here, there is no doubt whatsoever. Mr. Alvarez is guilty, and he knows it. Now it is time for you to tell him."

The jury was instructed on Thursday morning at 9:30. At 10:30, they returned with a unanimous verdict of guilty in both cases. After the verdict was read, the judge revoked the bail that had been set and ordered that Alvarez be jailed until sentencing which was set for three weeks from the date of the verdict. Alvarez was handcuffed by the Sheriff's deputies and taken to jail.

After the jury was dismissed, the victims hugged Jackie and left, joining friends and family. Jenkins shook her hand, congratulated her, and left the courtroom knowing justice had been done. Jackie was swamped by firm members who had come for the closing arguments and by Rosalind, Elanor, and Jorge. Josephine and Noni would meet her at home.

Will was unabashedly teary as he shook Jackie's hand. "Yikes," was all he could say without turning away.

The victims would receive police protection for the foreseeable future and, if necessary, they and their families would be relocated under a Witness Protection plan. As it turned out, it wouldn't be necessary.

Three weeks later, Alvarez was sentenced to two terms of 18 years in prison for each of the crimes. The sentences would not be concurrent and there would be no good time off for good behavior. Thirty-six years in prison – Alvarez would be a very old man when he got out.

With Alvarez gone and his gang depleted by Officer Jackson in the shootout, the rest of the members walked away from him – some to another gang in the War Zone and some to look for a better way to live. In the years to come, some would live and some would die. But between Jackson and a jury, notice had been given.

Chapter Twenty Eight

Update

In early December, the Mayor, D.A. and Chief of Police held another press conference. The Mayor, to her great credit and smart politics, announced that the backlog of 5,000 cases had been reduced to just under 1,000 cases and then turned it over to the "people who had made it happen, the District Attorney and the Chief of Police."

Each, in turn, thanked and praised their staffs and, in particular, Lieutenant Sheila Jackson for her hard work and the Sexual Assault Strike Team for its willingness to volunteer so many hours to help the cause. They also recognized the 'Motown Five' from the Lab who had been invaluable to getting the tests run. What was not announced was the going away party for the 'Motown Five' at the Lab that, in the aftermath, had taken several days to clean up, especially the beakers that needed to be sanitized of the tequila they had held. Begrudgingly, the head of the Crime Lab from Detroit had announced she would take them back for another six months as Detroit had now become the national leader of untested rape kits.

The news that day was not all good. The week before, there had been reports of twelve sexual assaults in the greater Albuquerque metropolitan area alone.

What was important was that each of the victims had undergone a rape kit test at one of the local hospitals to collect the DNA to send to the Lab to be tested. Each of the victims was promised follow-up by the police and the promise was kept.

Epilogue

Her pension vested, Alicia Robbins retired at the end of the year and moved to California. She was never heard from again.

Lieutenant Sheila Jackson was appointed Chief of the Sex Crime Unit of the Albuquerque Police Department after her predecessor retired at the end of the year. He was never heard from again.

A bladesmith from Belin, New Mexico, designed an ankle knife sheath and donated them to the Albuquerque Police Department. Almost all the women patrol officers and most of the male officers took advantage of it. Sheila Jackson, although now off the streets, wore one in honor of Jackie LaPointe.

No one was ever arrested in the deaths and disappearances of those perpetrators who were never charged because the victims wouldn't co-operate. Evidence of a vigilante group was never proven although the police, including Margaret Espinosa, could never believe the deaths and disappearances could have been done by just one person.

No one was ever charged in the castration and death of George Duncan whose DNA was connected to the rape of Leslie Helm.

This one-time justice was not forgotten.

About the Author

This is Bill's seventh novel. The only good thing that came out of the pandemic was the advent of Zoom and that allows him to practice law remotely. His office is still in Michigan but most of his time is spent in New Mexico with his wife, Rebecca Sitterly, their dog LacyB and 4 cats. Land of Enchantment.